THE STRUGGLE OUTSIDE

OTHER BOOKS BY RAYMOND FRASER

fiction
Bliss
The Madness Of Youth
Repentance Vale
The Trials of Brother Bell
In Another Life
The Grumpy Man
In A Cloud Of Dust And Smoke
Costa Blanca
Rum River
The Bannonbridge Musicians
The Black Horse Tavern

memoirs, essays & stories
When The Earth Was Flat

biography
Todd Matchett: Confessions of a Young Criminal
The Fighting Fisherman: The Life Of Yvon Durelle

poetry
Before You're A Stranger
Macbride Poems
The More I Live
I've Laughed And Sung
Waiting For God's Angel
Poems for the Mirimichi

THE STRUGGLE OUTSIDE

a novel

*Revised edition with an
Afterword by the author*

Raymond Fraser

Lion's Head Press

The Struggle Outside was originally published
in 1975 by McGraw-Hill Ryerson. In 2011 it was revised
by the author and published in a two-novel set under
the title *The Trials of Brother Bell*. This is a separate
edition of that revised version. The Afterword is published
here for the first time.

The author would like to thank the New Brunswick Arts
Board for a Creation Grant awarded during the writing
of the book.

Cover picture by Paul-Emile Boutigny

Library and Archives Canada Cataloguing in Publication

Fraser, Raymond, 1941-, author
The struggle outside : a novel / Raymond Fraser. --
Revised
edition with an Afterword by the author.

Originally published: McGraw-Hill Ryerson, 1975.
ISBN 978-1-928020-02-8 (pbk.)

I. Title.

PS8561.R3S8 2014   C813'.54   C2014-902447-9

Lion's Head Press
Toronto • Canada

CONTENTS

PREFACE

Contained here is the definitive account of the origins of the revolution presently engulfing New Brunswick. Since my capture several years ago I have been kept in close confinement, and having no way of knowing precisely when the culmination of our struggle will be reached I wish to have the enclosed history published so that it may be distributed throughout the country—and in particular reach those valiant members of the underground who are still engaged in the struggle.

This is not the first time my enemies have laid hands on me. Once before I was brutally and illegally detained and—along with numerous other political prisoners (those considered especially dangerous)—confined to an insane asylum; a common practice in political systems based on terror and corruption.

While imprisoned this way I encountered certain others suffering the same fate, and together we concocted a plan of escape. Once free, we vowed, we would ignite the powder keg of discontent that was so manifest in our native land; we would set off the revolution so long overdue.

There were six of us: my closest collaborator, the man through whom I secretly worked (for reasons you will see in my narrative), Chief Magaguadavic; Angus Moses; Elizabeth Werner; Cyril Cavanaugh; Philias LeBlanc; and myself.

These, I hoped, would be the core of the revolutionary army.

Of the other five the only one I knew to any degree at the time of the escape was Chief Magaguadavic. Our comradeship (now at an end, due to his subsequent treachery) came about as the result of a common passionate interest in overthrowing the regime that had put us where we were. It was through my inspiration that he recruited the others. For tactical reasons I preferred to remain in the background for a period and so kept aloof from the other four, scarcely speaking to them until we were all at the Farm, our first HQ.

It is not necessary to reveal the details of our escape (some aspects of it may still be put to use in a future attempt) but there was a certain amount of violence committed by Moses, to whom violence and cruelty seemed a natural way of life (I had heard it said, though at first I thought it simply a rumour—I believe it now—that he had in the past put his children's hands into a gas flame to punish them). In the dead of night the six of us broke out and separated with an arrangement to meet in Fredericton, the most likely centre from which to carry out our plans of revolution.

As it happened I was the last to arrive there, more than a week after the others. The car I hitched with was going all the way to Montreal and at the time that city seemed a secure place to hide for a few days (there was some confusion and anxiety following the escape). Reaching Fredericton from there, however, was another story. I had only a few dollars and a difficult time of it getting drives. Fortunately the others didn't give up on me. When I reached the capital Liz was waiting at the appointed meeting spot, the Beaverbrook Art Gallery. By then they had moved out to an abandoned farm that Moses knew of; while in the Army he had been stationed at Camp Gagetown for a time and he was familiar with the area. They'd stolen a car, broken into a second-hand sporting goods store and loaded up with camping supplies, several weapons and ammunition; walked off with a supply of dynamite from a construction site; and commandeered an outboard motorboat.

It is at this stage that my narrative begins. I have chosen to write in the present tense, in the manner of a combat journal, hoping this will bring the story more vividly before the eyes of the reader.

You may wonder after you've read this history what became of the Chief and Moses and Liz and LeBlanc, and if Cavanaugh survived or not. All I can tell you is I don't know. They keep everything from me here; they lie to me constantly. I have the greatest difficulty getting information on the state of the revolution—or about anything else for that matter.

You have received my manuscript because I was able to get it smuggled out; there is a young sympathizer who is being released tomorrow, and he promises to deliver it to a publisher. He assures me he will be travelling to Toronto before long.

I ask that all proceeds from the book be turned over to the acting command of the Popular Liberation Party to help hasten the day of victory.

I believe that is all that need be said.

CHAPTER ONE

Liz

There's a footpath by the stream cutting through thick underbrush and we follow it inland. It's a rough little path, wet and mucky in places, and once my feet are soaked I stop trying to bypass the bad stretches and follow Liz's example of walking straight on, over my ankles in mud and water. Some minutes later we come to a rope bridge spanning the stream which at this point is about forty feet across. The bridge lies hidden around a bend so that you come upon it suddenly.

"This is *only* for an emergency withdrawal," she says. "Once across you can undo it with a pull of the rope, haul it up and hide it. Do you understand that? There'll be no evidence that we crossed here providing we have any kind of start. The water's deep here. Do you want to try crossing?" Her voice is high-pitched, almost hysterically shrill and very annoying to listen to.

"Sure."

"I'll go first." The bridge is attached to a thick spruce on this side and Liz pulls herself up the base of the tree and climbs onto the ropes. It's a simple bridge, one length of rope to walk on and two lengths waist-high for handholds. As she moves forward it jerks sharply from one side to the other. When I start up the tree to follow her she snaps at me over her shoulder: "*Wait* till I'm across, *please*, it rocks like crazy with two people on it." So I wait until she's reached the other side. "Now you can come," she says.

I cross over, taking tiny cautious steps and being bucked about like a puppet. When I climb down on the other side I say, "It's pretty slow for an emergency."

"We'll need to practice. The Chief and Moses can get over very quickly."

"What about Cavanaugh?"

"Don't mention him! That man's used to groping around, he can manage to *feel* his way across. Anyway it would be no loss if he fell in. He's not completely blind anyway. Did you know that?"

"How blind is he?"

"I'm not sure. He says about ninety percent. But I'll bet he sees more than he lets on."

"Has he tried to cross yet?"

"No. Moses built it only a few days ago. Moses was in the army. That's where he learned it. He's so stupid though."

"Well, his army training should come in handy."

"It might if he wasn't so *stupid*!" She's holding a rope in one hand. "This is the rope that releases the bridge so don't pull on it."

Where we are standing clusters of leafy young birches grow out of the bank and hang over the water. They're as high as our shoulders. "What happens when we get across? Where do we go from here?"

"There's a cache of food and ammunition further back. I'll show you where it is. Do you want me to show you where it is?"

We start to move into the woods when she stops and points back across the stream. "That path we followed continues upstream," she says, "and there's a trap further up so *don't* go walking there."

"What kind of trap?"

"A pit! Moses dug a pit and covered it with leaves and things. It's three or four feet deep and it's filled with water. It's meant to delay our enemies and make them wonder what's going on. That's what it's *meant* to do. If we're chased and we cross the bridge and pull it after us and hide it they should keep right along the path and fall into the pit. Isn't that funny? They're supposed to be deceived into thinking we went *that way*. Personally I don't think it's much use." We set off into the trees. "Before you go walking by yourself you'd better have a talk with Moses and get him to show you around. He's made other traps all over the area. I don't know where some of them are myself."

"Well, he's enterprising, Moses."

"Do you think so? At least it keeps his small mind occupied. He's such a ridiculous person."

For about twenty minutes I follow her through the bush getting hot and sweaty as the sun flares through the tree tops, until we come to a little clearing.

"Well," she says.

"Well."

"We're here."

I look around. "I don't see anything."

"That's the way it's supposed to be, stupid." She brushes aside a low branch of a spruce tree and points. I can see nothing but a normal forest floor covered with orange-coloured needles and a few twigs. "It's a pit," she says, "you have to sweep away the needles to get to the hatch. Underneath are the supplies."

"Oh. And what after this?"

"After this we just have to do the best we can, that's all. We'll march deeper into the woods and regroup ourselves. Moses has taken several hikes further along and claims he's found a few places where we can safely put up temporarily, until we get a chance to cross the river or the highway. He says they are concealed places with vantage points. Do you know what a vantage point is?"

"The Chief says we ought to find more

locations like the Farm, just in case," I say. "Only even better hidden."

"Naturally. But we don't have all the time in the world, you know. It will all get taken care of later. Are you afraid? Do you have a cigarette?"

"I smoke a pipe."

"I hate pipes. Let's go back."

"Can you swim here?" I ask. We've crossed back on the bridge and are retracing our steps along the path. "I mean do you ever swim in the stream here?"

"Yes, I've done it. The water's cold. There's a good spot further along."

"I wouldn't mind a swim. That sun's some hot."

"Whatever you like. But you'll freeze. I think I'll have a swim myself."

"Well, I guess you'll freeze too."

"No I won't. It won't bother me. Cold water doesn't bother me at all."

"Then it won't bother me either."

"Yes it will."

The stream is flowing fast beside us, gurgling over rocks, and in the calm backwaters long-legged insects skim over the surface. A few swallows swoop back and forth after flies. We come to a bulge in the stream. The near bank is clear and pebbley and on the other side there's a pool of dark water. "This is the place," she says. "It's more than eight feet deep over there!" She delivers this, a simple enough statement, with shrill ear-piercing vehemence. It's a difficult voice to get accustomed to; and the way she looks at me with staring astonished eyes, it's beginning to make me feel uncomfortable.

"Well, let's get in," I say.

But already she's thrown off her bush shirt and she steps out of her pants and she's standing there with only a pair of frayed panties on. Peeling these off she suddenly shrieks; "Did you say something?"

Jumping back I reply, "No, I didn't say anything."

"What are you staring at?"

"I'm not staring. I see you didn't bring your bathing suit."

"Does that offend you? You're afraid to look at me! Ha ha! You're blushing!"

"No I'm not." Of course I'm trying not to.

"Yes you are!"

I mutter a few unintelligible words and slip out of my clothes and follow her into the water. I don't have to pretend it's cold, all I have to do is look at my feet: they're turning blue. There are hard little pebbles underfoot and I wince with each step. The water doesn't go above our knees all the way across until we reach the pool on the other side, and then it drops off abruptly. I stand on the brink rubbing my goose pimples, legs numb from the knees down.

"What are you waiting for?"

"All of a sudden I'm not hot anymore. This is ice water."

"I told you! As you can see it doesn't bother me. I don't feel it at all."

"I think I'll do this gradually." Reaching down I wet my hand and touch it to my thigh. With a contemptuous look she slips forward into the deep pool and surfaces slowly and does a sidestroke to the other side. Then she swims back to the middle of the pool and treads water, watching me as I pat my belly with a wet hand. "All right, all right, I'm coming." I count to three and close my eyes and fall face down. In a flash I'm out and standing on a flat rock on the other side. "Get out quick... before it freezes over," I gasp.

"It was *much* colder a few days ago! Haven't you any courage at all? It will get better if you stay in a while."

"Yeah, sure." But I make a show of gritting my teeth and jump in. It's still none too comfortable but after paddling around for a while I get somewhat accustomed to the temperature. At least I'm no longer bothered by the heat.

There isn't much room in the deep water for the two of us; we swim around each other for a while and then climb out and sit on the table-like rock and dry off. The sun's warmth soon calms my shivering and the goose pimples disappear.

I glance briefly at Liz, then look away. Without clothes she looks not much worse than many other girls; her legs and hips are on the heavy side and her closely cropped head seems unusually small, but if she were in any remote way charming... how should I act? Certainly I would be tempted—but she's not charming, that shrieking voice of hers and those bizarre staring eyes should be enough to frighten off a drunken sailor, let alone a man as seemingly timid and awkward as myself. I wonder if she's always like this... or is she only putting it on, testing me, trying to catch me off guard... but she couldn't possibly suspect who I am, I've been very careful...

I sit there passively and for a few minutes neither of us says anything, and I become conscious of the tranquility around us, the faintest of breezes in the trees, the stream rippling over rocks, some birds far off chirruping. This is suddenly shattered by the banshee cry of Liz exclaiming: "Will you please stop looking at me out of the corner of your eye! I know what you're thinking!"

"What?—what am I thinking?"

"You think I'll let you! Just because the both of us are in the nude! I'm not stupid you know!"

"I'm not—" The very thought makes me shudder. "I'm not thinking about anything at all," I say. "Honest."

"I'm sorry, but you are! You don't have to tell me lies, it only puts a black mark against you. Just because I have a body that arouses your desires doesn't mean you can take liberties with me. Do you hear? I said do you hear!"

"Yes.

"Please don't touch me. I did not give you permission to touch me."

"I didn't touch you."

"I saw your hand moving."

I looked down at my hand. "I didn't see it move."

Her wide astonished eyes stare at me. "You are such a *hypocrite*. Will you try to be honest with yourself ? You know there's nothing wrong with sex, you don't have to be afraid of your desires. Please have the guts to tell the truth. Go ahead, *tell* me, don't be afraid. Tell me what you want!" This last is screeched threateningly at me. I think, there seems to be no other avenue, but I don't see how— "Oh well, if that's what you want—"

"What I want? You make me laugh! I'm sorry to tell you, little boy, but for all your erotic desires you'll get nothing from me. I'm not in the mood today and moreover I find you very unattractive. I might even say repulsive! You don't even look like a man. Look at that!" She points.

She's really going too far. "What's wrong with it?"

"That's *enough*. I can't stand males who talk about nothing but sex! You're puerile. You make me yawn." She simulates a yawn. "What a bore you are. A bore and a hypocrite and a homosexual."

"Listen now—"

"A BORE and a HYPOCRITE and a HOMO-SEXUAL and do you know why I know this? Because you're STUPID. And if you make any advances towards me you'll regret it."

I make a gesture of despair. "You win, I won't try anything."

"Did you say something?" Her saucer eyes look at me incredulously. "I wish you wouldn't interrupt me while I'm speaking. It's impolite and shows you have an underdeveloped mind."

The rock is beginning to feel rough and hard beneath me, and needless to say I'm not overly entranced by the conversation; I suggest we go back to the Farm.

"We'll go back when I say so," she replies placing firm emphasis on each word.

We remain several minutes longer in the sun. Liz falls silent and lies on her back with her eyes closed. She raises one knee lazily. I think, "After everything she's said—is she waiting for me to do something? But it doesn't matter, I'm not going to. It doesn't match my character... I'm not so forward as that... If Liz *is* what she appears to be I'm already learning vital things about her... It means I've chosen the proper strategy... It's the only way to make an accurate assessment, and it shouldn't take long. Unless the Chief betrays me... But why should he do that?"

"I'm going back. You can stay here if you like since you seem so fond of the place." She gives me a scornful look and plunges into the water.

"Do I have to get back into that, isn't there another way across?" I ask.

Standing in the shallow water beyond the pool

she says, "Not unless you'd rather walk to the rope bridge."

I don't want to do that. There isn't even a path on this side. With resignation I leap into the water and surge out on the shallow side immediately. "Now we're all wet again," I say wading ashore.

But it doesn't bother her, she pulls her clothes on and slips into her sneakers and walks on ahead without me. I dry myself as best I can, using my shirt for a towel, and get dressed and set off after her.

When I catch up she says, "Do you know how to cook?" Her attitude is now that of haughty disdain—or so she must imagine.

"I can boil potatoes—fry an egg—heat a can of vegetables—"

"Then you'll have to take your share of cooking. I refuse to do it all. The Chief is often away. Moses is a total slob in the kitchen, he won't wash his hands or the dishes and the food he prepares tastes like garbage. I needn't even *mention* Cavanaugh. Or that other moody creature. So I've had to do almost all the cooking myself and it's not fair."

Moses

Liz has described Moses as coarse, brutish, unmannered, vulgar and uncouth. It doesn't take long before I accept her description as fair and moderate. He's about thirty-five and a massive bear of a man who's seldom without a scowl or a snarl—except when he finds something amusing; at these times he displays a harsh and vicious laughter.

When I return with Liz he thrusts a rifle at me, almost knocking me over. It's a Lee-Enfield .303.

"Know how to use this?"

"No."

"Hah! That's what I figured."

"Maybe you can show me."

"Show you, eh? What're you doing here if you can't use a rifle?" He grabs it back from me, rips it out of my hands.

"I can always learn."

"Hah!" He stomps out the kitchen door and without looking back says, "Get out here."

I follow him into the yard and he roughly and impatiently gives me instructions. The use of a .303 is simple enough, a matter of loading and attaching a magazine, cocking the rifle by working the bolt, aiming and pulling the trigger. To fire another round repeat the bolt action. Simple. But I have him show me several times.

"Okay, you got that now. But it don't mean you can hit anything. You got to aim and hold'er steady and pull the trigger real soft. Lemme show you how it's done."

He takes the rifle from me and inserts a loaded magazine and looks around him. Then he raises it and says, "See that cat over there?"

A tiny black and white kitten is snooping

around in the grass by the barn, making little leaps at insects.

"You're not going to shoot that, are you?"

"Why not?" He continues to sight along the rifle barrel.

"I don't know. It doesn't seem necessary... It's only a kitten."

He laughs at me hoarsely. "You're going to make some soldier," he says. "Alright then, if it makes your little heart bleed we'll use another target. See that tin can over there, by the door. Go put it on the fence."

I pick a rusted can off the ground and walk to the corner of the barn where there's a fence partly enclosing a manure compound. There's no manure in it now and the fence is falling down, just as the barn is gradually decaying away. It's an old farm; it must have been abandoned a long time ago.

My hand is barely removed when the can goes rocketing into the air and the report of the rifle rings in my ears. It's followed by Moses' laughter, if you can call his crude guffawing laughter, and he says, "That's how it's done, see. Nothing to it."

I walk back to him and say, "You've got a great sense of humour."

"Scared you, eh? Well you better get used to bullets flying around or you're in the wrong outfit. Here, take this." Passing me the rifle he places the can back on the fence. "Don't you try no foolishness 'cause you ain't a good shot like me. Wait'll I get back there."

The temptation is hard to resist but I hold my fire. There'll be another day. He returns to my side. "Now, you got a better chance of hitting it if your elbows is resting on something. The best way is to lie down. Here, get down on your stomach." He positions me on the ground, body angled and legs spread, elbows planted solidly. "That's the proper way, see. I learnt all this in the army. Get the can in your sights and don't shake the rifle and squeeze the trigger slow, don't jerk on it." I do as instructed, and the rifle blasts off in my ear. The can remains standing in its place.

"Didn't figure you'd hit it."

"Will I give it another try?"

"No point in it, you'd never hit that can, you're only wasting ammunition. Besides it makes too much racket and there might he a warden or someone sniffing around." He unloads the rifle and gives it back to me and says, "Practice holding it and aiming and squeezing the trigger slow. I can't waste my time with you no more, I got things to do."

Cavanaugh

Cavanaugh has a notebook and pencil in hand, held within an inch of his thick glasses and he's painstakingly writing something down. There's a crude hand-hewn bench against the wall outside the kitchen, it's in the sun and Cavanaugh's sitting there. I go over and sit beside him and take off my shirt. The yard is largely overrun with grass and weeds and there are a lot of white moon-shaped dandelions, the kind that get blown about in the wind like little parachutes. I absently watch a yellow butterfly fluttering around the wood tops. The sky is a vast empty plain of blue.

Sensing me beside him Cavanaugh says, "I've got you down in here." He sniggers. "This is my journal, I started keeping it the day I got here, I plan to write a book when all this is over. We're living important history now."

"Are there any fish in the stream?" I'm thinking about the half-rotten hamburger we had for dinner. There's no electricity at the Farm and of course no refrigerator.

"Oh I think so," says Cavanaugh. "Yes, we've caught some trout,"

"Do you suppose I could catch a trout?"

He is finished with his journal now and returns it to the small knapsack where he keeps it. "I don't see why not. I've caught one and if I can I suppose anyone can. We have a rod here. I'll come with you if you like."

We get the rod and Cavanaugh shows me where to dig for worms. There's a place in the yard where the earth is overturned and a shovel with a broken handle is stuck in the ground. I overturn a number of sods cutting several worms in half in the process and in a while have what I estimate to be enough, about a dozen. "Put some earth in with them," says Cavanaugh. He is bending over peering hard into the worm can. I do as instructed (for I probably haven't fished in my life) and we trudge down the grassy bank to the stream. "This may not be the best location but it's where I caught mine," says Cavanaugh. "You can try here anyway." The rod is about six feet long and there's a reel on it. I take the bare hook in my hand. "Time to put a worm on," I say. I try to shake one out of the can and a whole knot of them come together all wrapped up among themselves. I get my fingers onto one and tug and he comes away reluctantly. He immediately stretches out long and thin as a thread. He isn't as big around as my hook now. I drop him on the ground. "Better try another one," I mutter. "What?" says Cavanaugh.

"Nothing, just looking for a good worm." I get the hook onto the next one all right. When it hits him he jumps and begins squirming in a panic and dark rusty blood pops out of his skin. I shove his squirming body onto the hook until I have him bunched up like an accordion and the hook comes out near his tail—or his neck depending on which end I started at. "Now," I say.

Letting some line out I toss it into the water thinking that this is good practice for me, a harmless endeavour like fishing, to do as characteristic job as I can—even before a blind audience. The hook lands about three feet away. Naturally I've seen pictures of men fishing and observed how they'd whip an arm forward and arc the line out over the water. So I try that, giving myself more line. It's a poor parody of a cast but I get the line about five feet offshore and leave it there. After a few minutes I say, "There don't seem to be any fish here."

"But you haven't tried very long. I might remind you that a fisherman's principal virtue is patience," says Cavanaugh.

I pull the line in and flip it out again (who's to say that Moses is not secretly watching?), this time trying to place the hook further upstream where the current will drift it down. When nothing happens I try again. "No luck," I say.

"You've only begun, my dear. Keep trying. It took me more than an hour to catch mine."

"An hour?"

"Of course this isn't the best time of day, you'd have better luck in the early morning or in the evening. Reel your line in slowly. Don't lose heart."

I reel in slowly, throw it out again, reel it in again. "Is your worm still on?" says Cavanaugh. I'm standing on a rotted log at the water's edge and he's sitting back on the grass. I pull the hook in and look. There's just a little remnant of worm on it, the hook is practically bare. "They must've eaten it and left the hook alone."

I go through another performance of impaling a worm and on my next cast feel a tug on the line. It tightens and begins moving downstream faster than the current. "Got one!" I holler and with a quick jerk, pull a flapping and tumbling fish out of the water and over my shoulder and onto the bank where it narrowly misses Cavanaugh. "Gracious!" he exclaims.

"Well, there it is." I watch it flop around on the grass above Cavanaugh. "Now what?"

"Take him off the hook."

"He's still alive."

"Have you ever fished before, my dear?"

"No."

"Pick him up and take the hook out of his mouth." I approach the trout and bring my hand near him. He's stopped for the moment lying there panting. When my fingers touch him it would be hard to say who jumps the most, me or the fish. "Is he a big one?" says Cavanaugh. "Pretty big," I say. "But not too big. He's hard to get hold of."

"Catch him around the neck, that'll keep him still."

I wrap a hand around his body but the trout slips greasily out and flips and flops some more. It's with apparent difficulty that I finally get a grip on him clutching him near the neck and squeezing. That works because he stops resisting. His mouth gasps open and his gills flare up and down, he looks altogether terrified and helpless. I have him in my right hand and with my left I get hold of the hook which he's swallowed whole, leaving only the eye sticking out. I grasp this and try to tug the hook free.

"It won't come, it's stuck."

"Pull harder, my dear, try to ease it out the way it went in." Cavanaugh is leaning over my shoulder, one hand holding his glasses tight against his eyes.

"How do I know which way it went in? I don't know which way the hook's turned." I pull at it in a circular motion but it's caught fast. It occurs to me to cut the line and throw him back and I'm about to suggest this when Cavanaugh says, "Give it a really hard pull."

So I do, give one mighty jerk and the hook comes out with about three inches of guts on the end of it. The fish is quite limp and lifeless now.

"Did you get it?"

"Yes." I toss the body down on the grass.

"I said your luck would change. You have to be patient. Put another worm on."

Taking a piece of stick I scrape off the trout's guts and get another worm from the can and stuff him on the hook. There's fish blood on my hands and earth in my fingernails. I make a few more casts, such as they are, but I think, "Enough of this foolishness. One fish will have to do." I say to Cavanaugh, "I've had enough, I guess I'm not cut out to be a fisherman."

Reeling in the line I walk up the bank and sit down on the grass beside him. Cavanaugh, sitting or standing, looks to be a tall man, but that's merely an impression you get because of his raw-boned thinness. His most prominent body features are projecting knees and elbows. He has a straggly reddish beard and wears glasses that are close to an inch thick, though they don't seem to help him all that much. He used to be a chemistry professor at the University of New Brunswick and it's because of this background that he's been put in charge of demolitions, a decision made by the Chief, not me. I'm told he spends a good deal of his time in the barn constructing time bombs and dynamite grenades.

"Yes, my dear, I'd enjoy fishing more myself," he says when I join him on the bank, "if I had the vision to perceive better what I was doing."

For obvious reasons I'm curious about his handicap.

I ask him about it, how long his sight has been so limited.

"Gracious, for as long as I can remember." He gives a grave sigh. "I was always nearsighted, I was born that way. But it's worse now than when I was a child. I used to be able to see things a few yards away. Today I can see a few inches and even that not very well. Beyond those few inches there's nothing but blurred shapes and fuzzy colours."

I shake my head in sympathy. "They tell me you've got a doctorate in chemistry," I say.

"Yes, so I have."

"How'd you ever manage it—I mean it must have been very hard for you."

He smiles. "There were problems, yes indeed. But you see I'd developed an excellent memory over the years; I had to; of course this helped me, if I heard a thing once I remembered it. And I was able to read for a time providing I held the books close enough and with the help of these strong glasses. An intelligent man, a resourceful man, my dear boy, can accomplish almost anything if he puts his will to it."

"But the lab work? Wasn't it... dangerous, didn't you have to handle acids and poisons and potential explosives...?"

"Well, I succeeded in doing it, but admittedly theory is my strong point."

"Oh." Before I can pose my next question he says, "I know what you're thinking, my dear, but you needn't be alarmed. There's no danger. Explosives are really quite simple, anybody with the slightest knowledge could do what I'm doing. Gracious me! I certainly don't want to blow myself up. Nor you, my dear, nor any of the others. You can be perfectly content that I'm taking every precaution. I assure you, you have nothing to fear."

With that supposedly taken care of we sit silent for a few moments, when abruptly he starts giggling. I gaze at him curiously. "What do you think of Liz?" he says, his voice almost a whisper, his manner confidential. "Have you... um, how shall I put it... sampled her... heh! heh! you know what I mean... yet?"

The change of subject and his peculiar manner takes me slightly aback. Not quite certain what he means I say, "Have you?"

He continues to giggle. He turns his face to me, eyes magnified like pool balls by the thick glasses, and winks. "What do you think? Don't be misled by that innocent facade of hers. She's artful, little Liz, so coy and coquettish. But if you want the truth, my dear—" He looks stealthily around, as though he can see if

anyone is nearby. "The things we've done! My goodness!" He sniggers and giggles, his bony body shaking
all over. "I hope I'm not embarrassing you," he says
when he gains some control of himself, "but I know
you understand how it is, one man to another. Have
you experienced her yet, dear boy?"

"No.

"Don't let her demure and kittenish ways fool
you, she puts on a show of blushing modesty but
underneath, believe me, there lies a smoldering tiger
of a woman! Ah, Liz! I am very, very fond of her, I love
to tease her and make her blush, she's such a joy, truly
she is. And spirit? Spirit? I tell you she can give it as
well as take it. Perhaps, sometimes, yes, we may tease
each other too much, but then it's all part of love-play,
nothing more. At times though... yes, unfortunately Liz
sometimes has her moods and when they appear I
wish we had more than one woman at the Farm. I've
mentioned the subject to the Chief but he wasn't a bit
receptive. Naturally he's right, we're not here to cater
to our sensual natures, but say what you will a man
has his desires and they can't be ignored. Do you,
pardon me, do you yourself indulge in—how shall I
say it—oh dear! Never mind, I know this is
embarrassing, you're almost a perfect stranger after
all. I'm afraid to ask what you think of me. But frankly
there's no one else to talk to out here. Some fools
imagine that because I'm nearsighted and a scholar, a
man of culture as well as a front line soldier that I'm
not interested in the society of ladies, that I'm a... a

homosexual or something, What a ridiculous notion! If they only knew..." He commences giggling and shaking again. "I surprise the lovely creatures, they don't expect it." His tongue shoots in and out like a snake's. "Zoom! I'm right down on them before they know what's happening! It takes their breath absolutely away. That's the secret, my dear! Oh, oh." After a while his convulsive tittering subsides. "Ah well. But it's not all good times," he resumes. "I'm a complex person, I have many sides. We all do, it's true. Injustice is something I well understand, one views it better from my position. Prejudice, scorn, arrogance, mistrust. In many ways I'm like the black man, I bear a similar cross, you see the parallel? Virtually blind all my life and considered a second rate blundering cripple by a lot of ignorant bigots. But in the better sense of the word, who sees as well as I do? Insight, that's the sight that counts." He nods slowly, wisely. "The system, my dear boy, is rotten through and through. There's a privileged class, don't ever doubt that, and they control everything, the money, the power, they can tell the rest of us where to get off, lock us up if we disagree. They have the prestige, the money, the mansions and the servants, all the pleasures of the flesh their depraved hearts desire, and they'll stop at nothing to preserve the status quo. But these arrogant self-styled aristocrats will come tumbling down, we know that. Don't we, my dear? And those who fail to see it, you know what they are? Blind!" He chuckles. "I've opposed repression, I've tirelessly worked for the uplifting of the downtrodden. Revolution has been my life. Years on the barricades I've been, proselytizing, polemicizing, tractizing, marching, always standing up to be counted. Yet few know about this. I'm not a seeker after fame. If it were to happen, well... so be it. But it's neither here nor there." He pauses. "You heard about the movement I led at the university? The mixed-residence movement? I was deprived of tenure for my troubles. Oh yes. Tell me, would a person with invert tendencies do a thing like that, fight such a fight? But they've never broken my spirit. Have they, dear boy?"

Night Watch

Night comes and the Chief hasn't returned. In the kitchen by the fluttering sallow light of an old oil lamp Moses and Cavanaugh sit playing gin rummy. For the third or fourth time I hear Moses snarl fiercely across the table: "Are you gonna play cards or not?"

Cavanaugh is bent over the table like a bloodhound sniffing for the scent, his nose an inch from the cards. He looks up and says plaintively: "I can't make them out. Why don't we light another lamp?"

"Because I said so. We're showing too much light already."

"But I can't—What's this card, this one here?"

"It's the two of hearts. What's wrong, you blind

or something?" His harsh laugh fills the kitchen, then ends in a scowl.

"That's not funny," says Cavanaugh.

"You got no sense of humour. That's what's wrong with you."

"I have indeed a sense of humour—"

"And you're holding up the game. Cut the talk and play cards." He adds in a malicious undertone, "You crazy blind bastard."

"I heard that!"

'I don't give a shit what you heard. Are you gonna play or what're you gonna do?"

"I'm trying. My goodness!"

The night is warm and inside the house the air is stuffy. There are no screens and the doors and windows are closed tight to keep out mosquitos. For the greater part of the evening I sit in the shadows by the kitchen window smoking my pipe and saying nothing. They don't invite me to play cards and I don't ask. Around midnight Moses looks aside from the game and scowls at me. "You, numb-nuts," he says, "it's your watch, get out there and relieve Liz. And don't go shooting at ghosts. If you think someone's coming get down here quick and let me know."

"Right, sir."

"And don't act smart or you'll get your arse kicked."

It's a relief to leave the oppressive air of the house for the freshness of the night, and with rifle in hand I drift up to a spot at the edge of the forest where

I'm to act as sentry, and where I find Liz sitting with her chin on her knees and a shotgun resting against the trunk of a tree. She gets to her feet as though in a trance and without a word or look my way walks down to the house.

I sit in the place she vacated, beneath a gigantic pine tree whose fallen needles form a soft cushion. There are millions of stars out, they glitter through the branches of the pine, and the moon is almost full. I can easily make out the barn and the farmhouse with its kitchen window glowing dull orange, and at the foot of the sloping field there's the black ribbon of the stream.

I smile to myself, thinking who the others take me to be: the rawest of recruits, an untested idealist, a perfect novice to guerilla life, and I'm sure they expect me to react to a night watch with terror in my heart and horrible visions in my imagination. I might even be found cringing in the dark shooting wildly at phantoms. If so then mustn't I attempt it—at least to a point? I clutch at the rifle and look apprehensively around me, listening to the night sounds, and I say to myself, "Oh, oh! That's not just the stream I hear—someone's swimming across it!" And I peer hard trying to find the swimmer. My ears, meanwhile, are attuned to the croaking of bullfrogs, and I realize that some of the croakings—though good imitations—are not made by frogs at all. They must be signals! It's not hard, now, to detect a motion, to hear a dry twig crack, and I stare hard where I spotted a black-clad man move, and I pick out the glint of the moon on his knife. To the side of the barn behind an old wagon wheel a rifle barrel rises slowly and points at me...

Should I be shaking and trembling, and if so will I run down and raise the alarm, announce that we're being surrounded? But no—I don't dare be that incompetent; inexperienced and impressionable, but not an absolute fool. There's no one there.

It's a most peaceful night; why should I bother to pretend otherwise with no audience but myself and the forest and the stars and that falling-down old farm... nobody sees me. And there's a certain danger—why deny it?—in letting the imagination run free, no matter how strong your character. In the night it's possible to see and hear many things. I did think I saw a movement beyond the barn... over there. After that I more or less pay attention to my assignment: keeping alert for intruders and bearing in mind that I'll follow Moses' instructions to warn him if someone approaches. Yes, I must be reliable to some extent.

The lamp in the kitchen goes out and the house stands in silence.

At three o'clock, when I'm on the verge of going to rouse Moses who's to take next watch, the kitchen door opens and in the moonlight he comes up the rise towards me.

"Who's that?" I whisper.

"Don't point that damn thing. It's me. Who d'you think it is?" His voice speaks low but no less harsh than usual.

39

"You, I suppose." It has gotten gradually cold and damp. I remark this to Moses, my teeth almost chattering. He growls and says, "Well, watcha waiting for?"

"Nothing."

"Then get the hell out of here."

I leave him in the shadows of the pine tree and walk down to the house.

The back door lets me into the kitchen and I make my way in the dark to the next room, once a sitting room I think (there's a mock fireplace built onto one wall), and find my sleeping bag and crawl wearily into it.

Visitor By Night

I'm startled awake. There's a terrible commotion somewhere, a thumping and crashing and thrashing and a hysterical voice shrieks: "Get *away* from me! Get *away* from me! You creep, you despicable worm! How dare you try to—" And a small voice protesting weakly, "My dear, ah, my dear, do be kind to me, you've hurt me, my dear, sweetheart, I think I'm bleeding—"

I can see nothing in the dark, and for a brief moment I'm confused as to where I am. The tumult that rouses me is coming from one of the front rooms. In a minute a door slams and with my eyes becoming accustomed to the dark I can tell it's Liz. She drops her sleeping bag on the floor across the room from me and sits down on it. "The dirty animal!" she cries in her high-pitched voice. "He's a common sexual criminal and he ought to be put in prison."

"Oh." My head feels befuddled with sleep.

"Will you do something for me, whatever-your-name-is?"

"What?"

"Please go and KILL that Cavanaugh! Do you know what he did? Do you think I can take this every night, having that slimy beast crawling over me while I'm asleep? You heard him in there. You should have stopped him!"

"I didn't hear him... I just woke up when you started screaming."

"You're a liar! And will you be considerate enough to shut up and stop interrupting me. I know your type, you and that other animal. But I was prepared tonight, he thought I was sleeping, and I was lying awake, I was lying wide awake and I saw him slither into my room on his stomach like a snake. His tongue was hanging out and he was *naked* and he was drooling and groping all over the floor trying to find me. I could have laughed out loud. But I waited for him, I didn't say a thing. He thought he would catch me asleep and assault me *sexually*. The idiot! I felt his scaly hand touch me and then I lashed out and clawed his stupid face and pulled his hair and I punched him and kicked him. I made him *cry*."

"Oh."

"He makes me want to PUKE."

I hear what would be Cavanaugh fumbling around in another part of the house, and then there is silence.

"And you," she says to me, "I'm staying awake all night, so don't attempt anything, my boy, just don't attempt anything."

What can I say? What could anyone say to a person like her? I bury myself in my sleeping bag and with the certain feeling her hectic eyes are riveted on me nevertheless succeed somehow in drifting back to sleep.

Cavanaugh In The Morning

The sun slants through the dusty window and there is no sign of Liz. My muscles ache, and in particular my hipbones are sore from sleeping on the floor with no mattress. There's no carpeting on the floor, not even oilcloth, only rough uneven knotty wood. Indeed aside from myself and some spiderwebs there's not a thing in the room, not a stick of furniture.

When I've dragged myself together and got my clothes on and the sleeping bag rolled up I open the door to the kitchen. Sitting alone at the table is Cavanaugh, looking morose and introspective and gently fingering the side of his face. Etched down his cheek through his weedy beard and as far as his neck are the scarlet trails of four fingernails.

I say good morning to him and he mutters back at me, "Hello."

A fire is burning in the ancient wood stove, a rusty old thing abandoned with the farm, and a kettle is boiling on it. I set about making a cup of instant coffee, and I remark, as I stir the stuff, "Did the Chief show up yet?"

He doesn't answer so I repeat the question.

"Not yet," he says absently.

"I wonder why?"

"I don't know."

I join him at the table and sip my coffee. We are silent for a few minutes before he coughs lightly and says, "I believe—correct me if I'm wrong—I heard you talking to Liz last night. Quite late last night."

I shake my head. "Not me," I say.

He raises his eyebrows.

"My dear, I distinctly—"

"What you heard was her ranting in the same room where I was. I was only trying to get some sleep myself."

"Well, it's about the same thing, ranting, talking. The important point is, what did she say to you? You'll pardon my curiosity but I would like to know. You understand? Don't be afraid to tell me. Come now."

How he could have failed to hear every syllable she uttered with that voice of hers is more than I can understand. But I say merely, "I don't know what she said, I hardly remember. Something about you and her, you were having an argument or a quarrel, I was too sleepy to follow her. It was none of my business whatever it was."

He nods his head reflectively.

"My dear, when you say we were having a quarrel, look at this." He turns his face sideways to me so I can better see the scratches on his cheek. "I told you previously of her hidden nature, her veiled passions. You'll recall that I intimated something of this. Last night, believe me, my dear, last night... ah, me." He meditates for a moment. "Last night she revealed such a fierceness of raw unmitigated lust that it quite took me by surprise, to say the least." He lowers his voice. "You can keep a confidence, my dear, if I tell you something?"

"If you like," I say.

"The last thing I wish to do is embarrass Liz," he goes on. "I respect, yes and cherish her delicate modesty far too much for that, but I know this will go no further than the two of us. Am I right?"

"Yes, yes, whatever you like."

"You know my technique—" All of a sudden, in an abrupt mood change, he begins giggling quietly, then says, "you know my technique, my dear. I like to as they say, go down, to put it succinctly, and I am not boasting when I tell you there are few as accomplished at this art as myself. So down I went. And—I'm talking about last night, you understand—I remained there for heaven knows how long, and my dear, she loved it, how she loved it, how she carried on. Writhing and moaning as the flames of her passion grew—it was most gratifying. Never was there a woman at such a pitch as Liz last night. I tell you, words could never describe it. But then—" He puts his fingers to his cheek, and his voice crows sombre—"in the grip of this frenzy, of this pagan and primitive experience, so to speak, she became incapable of restraining herself and she clutched my hair in her hand—and pulled with all her strength! Oh! and with her other hand, at the very summit of her climax she raked her fingernails across my face—and did that sting, my dear, did that ever sting! See, can you notice the marks very much?"

"I can see them, yes."

"And when she'd done this she pommelled me with her fists and kicked me furiously with her feet—now I ask you, did you ever hear of an orgasm like that? Was there ever a woman with such savage passions? There never was. At first I was shocked and confused, indeed I was angry for she'd genuinely hurt me, and this happened when I was in the midst of such pleasure. What followed was unforgivable, it was ungentlemanly and for me totally out of character. I punched her. Yes, with this fist—" He displayed a bony little fist. "I struck her in the stomach. It was the wrong step to have taken, and for more reasons than its mere brutishness. It had the effect of making her hysterical and she began shrieking and screaming at me and accusing me of all sorts of preposterous things, like coming to her room uninvited and even—how absurd this is—trying to rape her, the dear child. In this state she threw on her clothes and dashed away, and that's when she came upon you, my boy, and God knows what all stories she related to you. She was not herself."

I say nothing to that.

"But all this will pass and be forgotten," he concludes, "a lovers' spat, only a lovers' spat."

LeBlanc

The stream that runs past the Farm has its mouth on the Saint John River, north of Fredericton. We are not far from the mouth but around a wooded bend and out of sight of the river.

Shortly after dusk we hear a boat, the sound at first like the buzz of a mosquito far away and humming thinly. Immediately we take up position on the hilltop and wait there, crouched behind a low rampart of logs that Moses devised, a kind of makeshift fortress heavily banked with earth overlooking the stream. Our arms consist of the .303, a revolver and a double-barreled shotgun. I hold the shotgun having had it thrust derisively at me by Moses with instructions to point it towards the northeast, and when ordered to, squeeze the triggers one at a time. Liz is on my left with the barrel of the revolver resting on the top of the log wall. Cavanaugh who is unarmed chatters nervously, his head jerking this way and that. "Does it sound like our boat? Is it our boat? Do you think it's the Chief? What do you think?"

Moses grunts at him to shut his mouth, not taking his eyes from the bend in the stream.

"What if they got him? He might have told them everything. Maybe it's the police. What if it's the army? What—"

"I said shutup."

"It's getting closer, listen, does it sound like our boat? Can you—"

"For *Jesussake* I'll shove this rifle down your throat—"

"He'll ruin everything!" cries Liz. "He always does."

"And don't you start—"

A small outboard motorboat drones around the bend and noses up onto the shore at the foot of the Farm. A man gets out and pulls the boat further up and then walks up the rise towards us, hands in his pockets.

"Who is it?" whispers Cavanaugh. "Is it the Chief?"

A low growl comes from Moses.

"It's only that frog."

"Where's the Chief?" screeches Liz. "Why are you alone? Where is he?"

The man is stocky and black-haired and at the moment has a deep frown on his face. His name is LeBlanc, the final member of our nucleus and a sullen and uncommunicative fellow from what I've seen of him.

When he reaches us he says, "I'm very piss off, me—" His accent is strongly French; sometimes it's hard to understand him—"I'm gone lie down and sleep!" He spits the words out bitterly, walking past us and making for the house.

"Listen, arsehole, where's that big redskin, what're you doing back here alone?" Moses starts after him and the rest of us follow.

"I don' know where dat guy is, 'ow should I know? Don' ask me."

"What in hell happened?"

"He disappear dat's what, 'e drive away and leave me and I never see dat guy again, *coliss*!"

"He run off with the car—that bastard—"

"No, I see da car but I don' see 'im, I see da car park on da street and it's lock and dere's no key and dat's all."

"How'd you get out here—"

"I 'itchhike! *'ostie*! I stand dere six hour, dose fucking guy dey see one of dem frog eh? on da road and dey don' wan' to get dere car dirty, eh? *Tabernac*! Six hour I stand dere!"

We reach the house and with an uncharacteristic burst of loquacity he babbles out his story, and there's an intensely sore look on his face. He says, "Dat Chief 'e let me out on da street and say 'e meet me in two hour and tol' me to go shop for da food, but dat guy 'e never come back, so I wait dere for five, six, seven hour, I sit in da park by dat art gallerie and I tink da cops dey begin notice me so I walk aroun' and come back and I do dis till it get dark, *tabernac*! and I don' know what to do den. I got no place to sleep and I wonder where dat Chief guy is, 'e say he be back in two hour and 'e's not back and it's ten hour later. Dat piss me off, for sure!"

"Oh my oh my—what did you do then, dear boy? It sounds dreadful!"

"What I do den I walk up dat big 'ill about five mile till I get to da wood and I lie down dere and sleep. Only I don' sleep 'ardly at all I almos' freeze to death, it was cold like 'ell, I got no blanket and I kep' waking up and I shake and shiver and everyting and dat's no fun, *coliss*! In da morning I walk way down again to da park and I stay dere most da day and no Chief and so I say da 'ell wit dis and start 'itchhiking and dose cock sucker Anglaise dey drive by me wit dere nose in da air and den I get a drive at las' from anudder French guy and 'ere I am and I'm mad like 'ell and dat's for sure *tabernac*!"

Fuming he gets his sleeping bag, muttering to himself, and starts upstairs to turn in.

"Aren't you hungry, my dear?" Cavanaugh calls after him.

"Naw, I ate dat bag of grocerie you tink I gone starve?" He closes the stairs door behind him and disappears on clomping feet.

"Now what do you suppose became of the Chief?" muses Cavanaugh.

"They captured him, of course," says Liz matter-of-factly. Then with a screech: "Don't be such an idiot! And *now* what do we do?"

"Pipe down, for Christsake. I'll tell yez what we do," says Moses. "We keep right on going the way we was going. I ain't surprised they grabbed him, I figured that's what happened soon's he didn't show up yesterday. But that don't matter 'cause I got 'er all worked out. I ain't gonna go into details tonight but in the morning I'll tell yez what's gonna happen—and how it's gonna happen."

"*You'll* tell us, and who do you think you are? You're not the boss. When did you start being the boss?"

"Shut your fucking trap. And get out there on watch where you're supposed to be."

Five minutes later, when she's screeched herself out, Liz slams the door behind her and goes up the rise to the big pine tree.

Moses Assumes Command

In the morning, in his customary gracious way, Moses assembles us in the kitchen and announces:

"Whether you like it or not someone's got to run this outfit and to save us a lot of trouble I'll tell you who it's gonna be. Me." His fierce eyes sweep over us. "And I don't want no arguing, 'cause if someone starts arguing I'm gonna thump them good. We done alright getting this far and losing one guy don't mean too much so I don't want to hear no wailing and lamenting about that savage. One man ain't that important, I don't care who it is, if there's anyone needed around here it's me 'cause I'm the only one who knows anything about this kind of stuff. The rest of you don't have no army training, you don't know one end of a rifle from the other and you'd be lost in two minutes on a march through the bush. For that matter you'd be lost doing just about anything, the whole bunch of yez. Now if you got that straight we might get things moving."

For the moment at least there's no outcry of objection, not even from Liz, who stares at Moses with amazed bulbous eyes as though she's looking upon some prehistoric monster.

"First off we need a car, that's the first damn thing, and then you know what we do next, we get at that little operation we planned which I'm gonna call by an army name. It's gonna be called a Snatch Party 'cause we once did a thing like that during maneuvers when I was in the army. So don't forget the name. And one other thing you don't want to forget and I'll tell yez for the last time, we don't need that big buck. Don't think about him no more."

"I will so!" Liz bursts shrilly out of her silence. "He's our leader, not you, and we have to rescue him! That's what we should be planning. I know what you're up to, you're overjoyed they got him because *you're* jealous of him, he's ten times the man you are—"

"Listen you crazy whore, if you don't want a

faceful of knuckles—" etc. For several minutes they rage at each other, accompanied faintly by Cavanaugh, pleading in his mild little voice, "Please, please, be calm, there's nothing to shout about, listen to me, I have the solution, if you'll just listen, please be calm—" he repeats this over and over until at length Moses, suddenly noticing him, snarls, "What? What're you muttering about, you scrawny bastard—"

"It's so simple. Just listen to me."

"What's simple?"

"Don't pay attention to him! He doesn't know anything!"

"Now be calm, *please*. It's an easy matter to rescue the Chief and we don't have to change one iota of our—what did you call it?—Snatch Party—oh my, a *snatch* party—anyway—"

"Get to the point, nitwit."

"We merely add his freedom to our list of demands."

"We got too many goddamn demands already."

"But it's more important to free him than some of the things we're asking."

"Naturally!" says Liz. "Anyone knows that!"

"Yeah, you ask too much and they'll start bargaining and next thing they'll be cutting back on the money. We got to get the money first of all, we can't do nothing without it, how're we gonna raise an army and buy artillery and supplies if we're broke—"

"Yes, yes, we've been through that before, but we'll concede on something else before the money."

Moses frowns. As Liz observed he's plainly anything but enthusiastic about rescuing the Chief—now that he's presumptuously elected himself our leader. But what can he do? Even someone as thick-skulled as himself can't avoid the sense of Cavanaugh's words. "My goodness, Moses, we can't get into the habit of deserting our comrades just like that. It could be you in there instead of him. I think you'd want us to rescue you, now wouldn't you?" Moses glares at him. He doesn't reply. "We'd better stick together," Cavanaugh says, "if we do there'll always be hope should they capture *any* of us."

After grumbling to himself Moses says, "I don't give a shit what you ask for, as long as we get the money."

"Oh, I agree," says Cavanaugh.

"Like I told you," Moses resumes, "the first thing we need is a car, and we're gonna get one this morning. I got 'er all figured out."

CHAPTER TWO

Brother Bell Gives Up His Car

We can see the highway through the trees about thirty yards below us with our roadblock of an old rotted tree lying across it. On the other side of the road the land slopes further downward towards the river and beyond the river there are rolling tree-covered hills for miles and miles.

For a while luck is against us. The first vehicle to show up is an old antique of a pickup truck. It draws quietly up to the barrier and an ancient little man gets out. Bent and shrivelled he takes hold of the log and with an interminable effort, tugging, dragging, pushing he clears it off to the shoulder. Wiping his forehead he looks slowly around and I hear him saying, "some... god... damn... bastard..." When his truck is out of sight Moses gives LeBlanc an impatient shove and sends him down to put the tree back. Next a station wagon full of children pulls up and we have to let that go too, and once again LeBlanc descends the hill and replaces the roadblock. Then a huge tractor-trailer comes charging along the road and with a lot of hissing and wheezing of air brakes rolls to a halt within inches of the tree. A burly man climbs down, tosses the tree aside, gets back into his truck and it starts off laboriously, its great weight struggling to pick up speed. When LeBlanc gets back this time he's panting and muttering darkly in French and eyeing Moses sourly.

"That's the one," says Moses. A gleaming red Buick draws up to the barricade and the driver pops out and walks to the tree. He looks around, as though for assistance, then with an annoyed shake of his head bends over to drag it away. "C'mon!" Moses bounds down the hill and LeBlanc and I charge after him, crashing through the bushes like a gang of desperados. The man is at first frozen to the spot, startled, but then he makes a bolt for his car. He gets as far as touching the doorhandle when Moses with his massive hand outreaching seizes him by the collar.

"Now, now, brothers, what's—"

"In the backseat, you!" While I hold the door open Moses heaves him in like a sack of potatoes and we jump in behind him. LeBlanc meanwhile has removed the roadblock and with squealing tires we speed off down the highway.

"Now how about that?" Moses gloats. "Hardly took a second. I told you."

I look at our captive. He's a pudgy little man, bald and pink skinned, and he's wearing a neat pin-striped black suit. He closes his eyes, opens them, and in a voice hoarse and powerful declares: "Brothers, you've caught me by surprise. Why have you laid hands on me? The Bible says you are either in Christ or in the Devil. Are you in Christ or are you in the Devil?"

A look of incredulity crosses Moses' face.

"You are either saved or unsaved, you are either saved, the Bible says, or you are lost. Praise Jesus, for those who walketh in sin—"

"What the hell's this? Where'd this bird escape from?"

"I tell you, brothers, the Bible says you are either on the way to heaven or you are on the way to hell. Think, my friends, before you act rashly, consider what you're doing. For if you are saved there is no judgment but if you are lost there's the fires of hell, eternal suffering. Brothers, I must know what this is all about, where are you taking me, and why? Is it a practical joke?"

"He sound like a crazy man, dat guy."

"He sounds like one of them goddamn holy rollers to me. Keep your eyes on the road and shutup."

"I do the work of Jesus Christ, friends. Jesus said, I am the door and if any of you enter it you will be saved. Jesus said that, my friends, I didn't say those words, those are the words of Christ Jesus who died on Calvary cross, who endured the rejection of man and the wrath of God—"

"Okay, cut it out."

"—and God himself turned his back on his son and when the Lord Jesus who knew no sin himself took sin upon himself for our sake—"

"I said cut it out."

"The Bible says that if a seed falls on barren soil—"

Moses grabs him by the necktie. "Who or what are you?"

"Be careful, brother, that's a good tie."

He informs us, not without some pride in his voice, it seems to me, that he's the Reverend Philip Bell, more commonly known as Brother Bell, pastor of the First Church of the Resurrected Living Christ at Stoney Brook, near Woodstock. "You might have heard my radio program, 'Join Hands With Jesus', every Friday evening at eight, a half-hour of—" He starts into another spate of biblical phrases, but is interrupted when Moses takes the pistol from his belt and slaps him lightly on the head with the barrel. The preacher yelps. "Praise Jesus, be careful what you're doing. That hurt."

We turn off the highway and follow a rutted barely discernible lane down the edge of a field and bounce our way into a poplar grove near the river. Here the car is perfectly concealed.

"Alright, let's go. Get moving." Moses roughly

pushes the preacher out of the car.

"Would you tell me—"

"No, I'll tell you nothing."

It's only a short hike through the trees to the riverbank where our boat is pulled up in some bushes. When we've got it shoved into the water Moses announces we are to blindfold Brother Bell before loading him aboard—"so if we ever let him go he won't know where he's been." He takes a greenish balled-up handkerchief out of his pocket.

"That won't be necessary, brother. I'll keep my eyes shut."

"C'mere. Turn around." He tugs at the sticky handkerchief until he has it more or less leveled out, cross-folds it once into a triangle then wraps it around Brother Bell's head. It covers his eyes but it also covers most of the rest of his face. Not surprisingly he retches and flings a hand up to pull it off. "No, you don't." Moses catches hold of his wrists. "We got to tie this bird's hands too, get me some rope from the boat." In a moment Brother Bell's hands are secured behind his back and Moses takes him by the arm and leads him into the river. "Climb in there, you." There's a muffled sound from the handkerchief. It's next to impossible for Brother Bell to climb into the boat by himself, blindfolded as he is and with his hands tied behind his back, so Moses grips him by the seat of the pants and hoists him headfirst over the side. He lands on his face with a thump: "Lord Jesus!"

"Quit your swearing," says Moses.

"Praise the Lord, I hit my chin on something. Help me up."

"Get in there, the rest of yez, and let's get going."

LeBlanc pulls the cord to start the motor and with the small boat low in the water we make our way upriver, keeping well in towards shore. It is now about eleven o'clock in the morning.

CHAPTER THREE

Arthur Manderson

Arthur Manderson is a lawyer, the son of a lawyer who was also the son of a lawyer—one of those, from a family of lawyers and politicians and crooks and, therefore, from quite a wealthy family. That had to be a consideration in my plans.

Not much more about him. Relatively young for his position, in his mid-thirties, easy-mannered, quick to smile; in the minds of most who bother about such things the undoubted heir to the premiership. Married to an attractive woman, daughter of the Toronto financier Richard Baillie, two children.

My information is sketchy, what I was able to pick up from newspapers and television, but more details are not important. I gathered enough to conclude he's our man, and informed the Chief of my decision, which he in turn relayed to the others—as though he had thought of it himself (as I instructed him to act).

Arthur Andrew Manderson, Liberal Member of the Legislative Assembly for York County, Minister of Justice in the Government of New Brunswick... His character is of no importance to us anyway, another insipid professional politician, a parasite, a product of the monied aristocracy, another front man for the powerful and vicious performing his duty of keeping the rich and the poor in their respective places, and dissenters under lock and key.

CHAPTER FOUR

The Chief

They must all be tested, and for Moses this will be the major test. But I meant for the Chief to lead the mission. Now it seems he is in their hands. The Chief... Magaguadavic... Peter Paul... He was christened Peter Paul on the Burnt Church Indian Reserve and changed his name to Magaguadavic when he was twenty years old because he refused any longer to bear a name derived from his race's conquerors... like a black slave bearing the name of his plantation owner master... but who can say a tongue-twister like Magaguadavic? So we call him the Chief. Sometimes I think it's strange that he works with us, for he seems to have little use for the white race. And yet he's my best lieutenant. It may happen that our nation will be divided at first—if he insists on a separate territory for his people—necessitating a general council of both territories formed to deal with external matters, military and economic affairs; but there are different ways to achieve the objectives of high principles, and the barriers will ultimately break down as our mutual trust grows, as we all come to accept that every human belongs to the one family....

CHAPTER FIVE

The Arrival Of Brother Bell

Brother Bell is still bound and blindfolded as we escort him up the rise to the Farm. All of a sudden in his raucous preacher's voice he breaks into song.

> *"Isn't it wonderful wonderful wonderful!*
> *Isn't Jesus my Lord wonderful!*
> *Isn't He wonderful wonderful wonderful!*
> *Isn't Jesus my Lord wonderful!*
> *Eyes have seen*
> *Ears have heard*
> *What's recorded*
> *in God's word—"*

He is starting into the chorus again when Moses hits him a slap on the head. The sound of the singing brings Cavanaugh tentatively out of the barn. Up by the barricade Liz has her owlish eyes fixed on us.

"What is it?" Cavanaugh's head is rotating nervously. "Liz, my dear, what's going on?" He's clutching a stick of dynamite in one hand.

Moses stops and looks at him for a moment. "That's dynamite, ain't it?"

"Yes, yes, but—"

"What're you doing with it? What in hell were you doing in the barn, how come you ain't up there at the barricade? Didn't you hear the boat? What if it was someone else? You don't sit in there working when you hear a boat coming."

"I know, I know, but I wasn't working. It was Liz's idea, she insisted I go into the barn, she wanted me to make myself useful, the dear girl. If it was an enemy I was to light a stick of trinitrotoluol and throw it at them. They wouldn't know I was in the barn, you see. While they were shooting at Liz I'd throw the explosive out the barn window at them."

Moses snorts. "A great chance you'd have of reaching them too. You'd most likely blow yourself up."

"Well, I'd do my best. And it would scare them. I think they'd go away quite quickly if someone started hurling dynamite at them. Who was that singing? Was that you, Moses?"

"No, brother, that was me, praise Jesus. Chained and led into captivity I raised my voice to the Lord. The Bible says, 'him who cometh unto me I will in nowise cast out, 'come unto me, saith the Lord, and if you care for your souls, my friends, remember it's not too late for salvation, for God says today to every sinner, come, come and I will receive you—"

"You're gonna come alright, you're coming with me while I tie you up somewhere that I can't hear you."

"Do you believe in God?" says Liz, astonished. "I don't think I believe in God. I wonder why you believe in God? What's he like? Where is he? Have you ever met God?"

The preacher stops to answer but Moses gives him a rough push towards the house.

"Who's he?" asks Cavanaugh of no one in particular. "Is he the Justice Minister? Did you get him already? He sounds strange... all that talk about coming. Dear me."

Liz Protests

"I want to go too! You can"t stop me, why can't I go if you can?"

"Because if they start shooting we don't want no hysterical bitch screaming and hollering and getting in the way."

"I do not scream! I do *not* scream! And I'm not afraid of shooting, and I'm not a bitch and I'm not hysterical and *you* are a complete idiot, and you'll make a mess of everything. You will! You don't have any brains. Can't you see that? It's so obvious to everyone else."

I say to her, "Somebody has to guard Brother Bell."

"Nobody's talking to you. Did I ask for your advice? Why don't you stay and guard him, why me and not you? Answer that question."

"I suppose I could," I say. They would expect me to say that, as though I'm afraid to go.

"Like hell you'll stay. I already told you you're coming and don't try to squirm out of it."

"I'm not trying to."

"Why *him* and not *me*?"

"Because I said so, and if you keep yelling at me I'm gonna boot your fucking arse. What difference does it make if you come or not? This ain't our only operation, we're gonna do other things—we're not playing a game, we're not going to the tavern, it's not like you're gonna miss a good time. Have some sense, for Christsake."

"I *have* got sense. If you won't take me along now, you have to promise I can go next time. Promise! You have to promise!"

"Yeah, okay. I promise. Next time."

"Hear that, everyone? You heard him. He made a promise and he'll have to keep it. He's so ugly—and so stupid! I know he'll make a botch of things, you watch and see!"

CHAPTER SIX

Infiltration Of The Enemy Stronghold

The drive south to the capital takes twenty minutes. The countryside of hills and trees in full leaf and planted fields and gray clapboard farmhouses yields to service stations, neoned motels, trailer parks, used car lots, billboards advertising automobiles, chainsaws, motorbikes, credit cards, hotels. Neither Moses nor I say anything. But LeBlanc, his sullen eyes staring over the wheel, keeps up a low steady muttering. As would be expected on such a mission my senses are exceptionally keen and alert and though his voice is almost inaudible I hear everything he says, as plainly as I hear Moses in the backseat behind me breathing like a horse.

"...dose governement men dey say LeBlanc go learn a trade we pay you to learn da trade yeah so I go to Moncton I learn da trade so now I'm mechanic apprentice and den I can't find no job *sacrament*... dey don' wan' no French guy dey got no job for da frog guys like us dey won't even let us shovel shit... me I come from da Baie and my fadder and brudders dey fish dere but dere's no money in dat you work like 'ell but you can't make no living fishing no more... yeah I tell you dat's gone change my fren' you don' push us roun' no more *maudit* bastard you got da big 'ouse and da big car and you got all da money and us guy we live in da shack and go on da welfare and our kids dere 'ungry and we're getting piss off... laugh at 'ow I talk dey say look at dat stupid guy he can't even talk h'english dat's one dumb guy we don't give him no job 'e's so stupid 'e can't even talk *coliss*... I fix all dem dat's for sure we're gone tak dose Anglaise dere gone eat some shit '*ostie* dose rich bastard dey don' laugh at LeBlanc no more and push' im aroun' dat's gone change quick for sure *coliss tabernac*..."

At times he crosses over into French, a French peppered with English, like, "je veux un job mais c'est trop hard de trouver—je vais to town pour faire shopping mais je got no goddamn money—"

It is two in the afternoon when we reach Fredericton. Since we've made our move so quickly we are fairly safe in our new car—it will be a while before Brother Bell is presumed missing.

"Pull up here," says Moses. "In there."

We are on the river side of Officer's Square, with its statue of Lord Beaverbrook standing in his chancellor's robes like a huge bronze toad. Off to one side is the old Officers' Barracks of colonial days, a wall of stone arches and balustrades facing us and shaded by three giant elm trees.

"Why are we stopping here?"

"I wanna think," says Moses.

"Haven't you made your plans yet?"

"Shutup."

"How are we going to locate him? We don't know where he is."

"I'm gonna find that out."

"How?"

"How do you think? I'll phone his house."

"Oh. Right. That's a good idea."

"You think I'm stupid or something?"

Being a politician it's unlikely Manderson would keep an unlisted number—he couldn't appear to be hiding from his constituents. When Moses returns from the phone booth he says, "He's in his office at the Legislative Building. That's what some woman told me."

"Well, do we go there now?"

"You're asking a lot of questions lately. She said you had to make an appointment, he's busy, she said. Only we don't have no time for appointments." For a moment he's silent, pondering.

"What'll we do?" I say. "There'll be guards."

"Lemme think a second. I seen this stuff in shows before. We can let on we're plumbers or something."

"Plumbers?"

"Lemme think."

After a minute he says, "Okay, I got'er figured, let's go. Drive till I tell you to stop, LeBlanc. I know this town."

At a glance it's a town of lawns and shade trees, elaborate gabled wooden houses, frequent stop lights, crosswalks and obedient pedestrians—plate glass store windows, dress shops, shoe shops, sporting goods, Chinese restaurant, movie theatre, barbershops, corner garage, tavern, parking meters, Woolworth's, Laundromat, Pizza Delight, Eddy's Hardware—at this last we pull to a stop.

"Wait here. Just a minute, gimme some money."

"I don't have any. Only a bit of change."

"Arsehole."

He goes into the hardware store and when he comes out he's carrying a green tin toolbox and a large screwdriver, and sticking out of his shirt pocket are a pair of pliers and a wrench. "Okay, go up around this way ...."

We drive along a quiet sun-mottled street and on Moses' grunt come to a halt by a pair of attached telephone booths, which he enters one after the other, jack knife in hand. He cuts both receivers off and with wires dangling gets back in the car. "Now let's go to work," he says.

§

The afternoon is sunny and windless and there are hordes of tourists milling around, aiming cameras and chattering, wandering from the Beaverbrook Art Gallery to the Beaverbrook Playhouse to the Lord Beaverbrook Hotel to the Legislature Building. The last is a solid brownstone structure with a pillared balcony over the entrance and a silver dome on the roof. The windows are narrow, arched and deep-set, and the main entrance faces lawns with rose-lined pebble paths and enormous flourishing elms, and below that the Saint John River. Across the corner from the Legislature is an ugly modern glass and steel structure where the government ministers have their offices.

To find a parking spot close enough we're forced to circle the block twice, creeping past the lines of cars parked bumper-to-bumper, until finally someone pulls out and we back quickly into his place.

"I'll do this myself," Moses says to me. "You don't see two guys going to repair a telephone and there ain't enough tools to go around—and you'd just be in the way anyways."

One of the phones dangles from his belt while the other is in the toolbox with the spiraled cord hanging out. He wears his windbreaker open so the pliers and wrench can be readily seen. He carries the large screwdriver in the same hand that holds the toolbox.

"I look like I come to work, now, don't I?"

There's no indication of any nervousness about him. Nor does LeBlanc seem in any way concerned. It seems unnatural. Are they both that courageous—or are they unable to comprehend the danger involved? It's broad daylight and the place is swarming with people.

"What door will you use? I don't think you should go in the main door."

"You think I'm a dummy? I'll find a door around the back." He checks the revolver, places it in the toolbox and gets out of the car.

Moses Gets His Man

Leaving the car Moses half-circles the building and suddenly chuckles to himself; up ahead there's a panel truck backed up to a side entrance. Two men are unloading boxes of some sort and with a nod he squeezes in by them. "How's she goin'," he says, like a man who uses that door every day. Inside he takes the stairs to the second floor and emerges into a long corridor. He stops a man with a briefcase and asks how to get to Mr Manderson's office. "I been told to get over here quick—telephone's out of order."

The man gives him directions and he goes up another few floors and along another corridor, and by reading the names on the glass doors reaches the office of the Minister of Justice. He opens the door and finds himself in an anteroom. Looking up at him from a desk is a wrinkle-necked woman with powdery white hair. She adjusts her glasses on her nose and says, "Yes?"

"Telephone company. I got to fix Manderson's phone, it ain't working right."

"Oh? Are you sure it's Mr Manderson? He's been using his phone all day—"

Moses meanwhile places the toolbox on her desk, raises the lid and removes the revolver. He says, "Don't open your mouth. I ain't fooling."

The colour drains from the lady's face.

"Anyone in there with him?"

She shakes her head, eyes transfixed on the gun.

"Okay, c'mon. Open the door. I'm right behind you."

"But—but—"

"Never mind the buts, do what I say."

He follows her into the inner office and pushes her aside, kicks the door shut with his heel and points the revolver at the Minister of Justice. "This is business, Manderson. Gimme any trouble you're as good as dead."

The Minister's eyebrows dart upwards. He gazes at Moses a moment. Then setting aside the sheaf of papers he's been going through he says, "I take it you're discontented about something. Have a seat."

"Fuck you have a seat. Get on your feet, over by that wall there."

Manderson lets out a heavy sigh. Then he smiles his engaging smile. "Something tells me this is going to be one of those days ...." Getting slowly up he comes from behind his desk and says, "This wall here? Do you want my hands above my head?"

"Yeah. Lean against the wall, put your hands up there against the wall and lean forward."

"Like they do on TV? Like this?"

"Yeah."

Moses gives him a rough frisking, finding no weapon but removing his wallet.

"Alright. Now stay there." He turns to the secretary. "Okay you, lie on the floor. On your stomach." As she does this, looking worriedly over her shoulder at the pistol, the phone rings. Moses picks up the receiver. "Hello... You got the wrong number." He hangs up, then lifts the receiver off the hook again, listens for the dial tone and places it on its side on the desk. Then using his jack knife he cuts the venetian blind cord from the office window and returning to the prone secretary ties her wrists behind her back and her ankles to her wrists, leaving her lying on the floor like a rocking horse.

"Now I don't want you making no noise when we leave," he says, "because if anything happens on the way out your boss is gonna get it. I'll empty this into him—" he wags the revolver in her face. "Understand?" She nods rapidly. "But just to be on the safe side I'm gonna shove something in your mouth." Hacking off a chunk from her dress he forces it between her teeth, stuffing her mouth until her eyes bug half out of her head.

"Well, Manderson, you and me is leaving now. I'm gonna be carrying my jacket and under it is this revolver and you heard what I said to the lady. If anything happens you get it and after you anyone else in sight. So just behave and we'll walk out the front door and go to my car. Don't stop to talk to no one. Understand?"

"Yes, certainly. Shall we go now?"

"Yeah."

With Moses at his elbow they leave the office and start walking down the corridor. They are about halfway to the end when a stoutly built man in a tweed suit pops out of an office and says, "Oh, Arthur, there you are. Can I see you a minute?"

"Oh... " He looks at Moses. "Can you make it later, Bill, I have to go with this gentleman."

The stout man gives Moses an up-and-down look, and says, "I see. Well, I'll just leave this report with Mrs Crosbie then."

As they set off in opposite directions Moses seethes through gritted teeth, "Tell him she ain't there!"

"What's that?" The stout man turns.

"I don't think she's in the office, Bill," says Manderson. The other man stands looking curiously at them. He is still rooted to the spot when they round the corner.

"Don't waste no time!" Moses roughly prods the Minister as they descend the stairs. At the bottom he jerks him to a halt. The entrance is blocked by men trying to squeeze a huge box through the door. He pushes the Minister along the passage and through another door and suddenly they're in the main floor lobby. At the end of it two uniformed commissionaires are standing with their hands clasped behind their backs, casually eyeing the coming and going of civil servants.

The Chase

In the backseat of the Buick I have my eyes glued on the pillared entrance, tense and ready to throw open the door and pull in our prisoner, should one materialize—a possibility that seems more and more remote as the minutes go by. If Moses were gone but thirty seconds the wait would seem interminable, but he's been gone fifteen minutes; at any instant I expect to see him bundled out in the grip of guards, and the orders are hovering on my lips: "LeBlanc get moving!" For we'll have to salvage what we can, to leave things in the hands of Cavanaugh and Liz would be unthinkable. I look at my watch. How much longer to wait until I give the order to drive off ....

We are parked in the sun and the heat in the car is suffocating. The motor idles and the front wheels are turned outwards and we're poised to burst from our parking spot—LeBlanc is mumbling again—

"...tell dat fucking frog dis is a white man's tavern 'e say dey don' sell no codfish 'ere—we should kick da shit outa dat guy making a joke of de Queen's h'english where'd you go to school you ignorant bastard 'ow come you ain't out in de pond wit da udder frogs 'e say..."

"LeBlanc—there they are."

The two of them have suddenly appeared at the main door and start down the steps, so close together they're touching. Manderson, tall and slender, walks briskly towards us, looking straight ahead.

"Get ready, LeBlanc."

"Yeah, yeah, I'm ready, *coliss*."

I open the door nearest them, feeling my heart pumping fast, marvelling that Moses actually succeeded—and then I hear a shouting, an excited voice calling, "Stop them—that man! Mr Manderson!" Running after them is a stout tweed-suited man, he's waving his arms and pointing and shouting, "Guards, police!" Behind him the two commissionaires dash out the door and down the steps.

Moses drops his jacket and the pistol flashes in the sun, and now he and the Minister are jogging towards us and Moses glances over his shoulder. He has one hand fastened to Manderson's sleeve. Just before they reach the car he stops, pulls his prisoner up short like a puppet, turns and without aiming fires a shot. At the crash of the gun the man in tweeds has a change of heart; with a jerk in his gait he veers off sharply behind a tree. There are scores of people around and the running and shouting and the gunshot sets off a general panic. Men and women plunge to the ground and scamper behind cars and trees and children are pulled at frantically. Amid the screams and mad scrambling the security guards themselves are quick to dive for cover.

"Quick!"

"Get in! Get in!" Moses hustles the Minister into the backseat then jumps in after him. Before the door is even shut LeBlanc wheels with a roar out onto the street and the car swerves and heaves as we round the first corner.

"Never mind the red lights. Mat 'er, god-dammit!"

We're on King Street and there are parked cars down one side of the street and several cars driving in front of us and others coming towards us. With his foot to the floor LeBlanc reels us through a scattering traffic disregarding stop signs and red lights, never turning his eyes sideways. Trucks and cars swerve and brake and fall away as we cut a swath down the centre of the street, bound onto the Woodstock road and past the hospital and the RCMP headquarters. Leaving the golf course behind we barrel down the open road.

I take a look at Manderson. He's laughing. Not hysterically, but an affable, quietly hearty laugh. "I don't know where we're off to but we should be there soon. Ho ho ho."

Moses leans over the front seat, above LeBlanc's shoulder, eyes on the road in front of us. "If they got a car between here and ..." He mutters... "fuckers'll block the road..." He turns and scowls at

Manderson, saying sharply; "You prick, you shoulda told that guy your secretary was out."

"Sorry, old man," Manderson smiles apologetically, "but you said not to speak to anyone. If you'd kept quiet yourself it's likely he'd have left the report on Mrs Crosbie's desk in the outer office—" The tone of his voice is cordial, ingratiating—"But on the other hand he might have checked a little further. I believe he was suspicious. So you're probably right. Next time I'll try to do better. Ho ho ho."

We're travelling at a reckless speed. The speedometer bobs around the 115 mph mark and it's not a straight highway, we yaw and skid on the turns, the car shakes and rights itself and in the backseat the three of us are repeatedly thrown against each other. Manderson has a faint, curiously amused smile on his face.

"I was wondering," he says, as we jostle about. "It appears I'm being kidnapped—I think that's a reasonable assumption, isn't it? Ho ho ho. But what I'd like to know is, why?"

Nobody answers him, we're too occupied watching the road behind and in front of us.

"You can tell me, surely. If it's a secret I'm good at keeping secrets. Ho ho ho. Is it ideological? Is there something we don't see eye to eye on? It can't be personal, I don't believe I know any of you gentlemen. It must be political. But why did you select me? All that risk you took, coming right into my office in the middle of the afternoon! I can't help but admire your nerve. You know, you'd have been better off with the Premier, he's far more important than I am. Or Watling, the Finance Minister, he's got twice the status I have—or at least he thinks he has. You wouldn't care to go back and try again? Ho ho ho. I guess not." Approaching a curve LeBlanc pulls out around three cars in a row, straining to catch the last one in the face of an onrushing tractor-trailer and narrowly slipping in ahead of it. "Whew! Close, that," says Manderson, settling back in his seat again. "Did it ever occur to you you're breaking the speed limit?... No?"

North of Fredericton the road from St Stephen meets Highway 2, the route we're following, and as we near the juncture—I see it ahead, an overpass and an approach road—Moses leans suddenly forward and hollers in LeBlanc's ear: "Drive 'er for Christsake the cops!"

"I don' see no cops, *coliss*! Ah—I see dem now."

They're coming onto the approach road, a two-tone highway patrol car streaking along in a race to head us off—they've a lead on us, they can get there first—if they're prepared to have us run smack into them. We can't possibly stop in time if they block the road. Prudently they slam the brakes and fan tail as we fly by and in a minute they're coming behind us, siren howling.

"Now what?" I say. "That's all they need, to keep us in sight and radio ahead."

"Shutup. Lemme think."

"Perhaps, you never know, if we stopped and

talked it over with them... ho ho ho." Manderson is looking hopefully out the rear window. "Believe it or not I have a certain admiration for you men," he says, "seriously. You must have genuine convictions to attempt a thing like this. I hope we'll get to have an exchange of views before long. You mightn't think it but I'm always prepared to learn something new. Of course this is hardly the time for a political debate ...." Turning from the window he looks Moses in the face. "Do you think... I mean, if we stopped and I had a few words with the police, that we might work something out? I'm afraid things don't look too good for you now. I'm quite sure I can convince the police... We could come to some sort of arrangement... It would be better for all of us. I'll give you my word now... You'll have your liberty, choose where you want to go. I *am* the Minister of Justice, after all. What do you say?"

"We ain't that stupid, Manderson."

"I think it's a fair offer. Believe me, I sympathize with men like yourselves who are dedicated to their principles, whether I agree with them or not. No shit. Before it's too late, you ought to—"

We haven't much time, we'll soon be at the road to the boat, if we have to go by that—

"Here, change places with me," Moses says.

"What?"

"Get over here. When we get out I want you in front of me."

"Oh. Certainly. Smart thinking."

They are both tall men and with the car reeling and bounding the way it is the transfer of positions is clumsily achieved. For a moment Manderson is sitting on Moses' knee.

"Well, that was fun," says Manderson. He's now seated by the door directly behind LeBlanc. "We'll have to do it again some time."

"Yeah." Moses lets out one of his crude laughs, reaches across the Justice Minister and flings open the door.

"What... My God don't do that!" Manderson's composure suddenly disappears, a shadow of horror crosses his face and his mouth begins to tremble. An awful comprehension pervades him. He struggles grasping at the side of the door, clutching at Moses; but he's taken by surprise and his desperation is not a match for Moses' brute strength. The air sucks him out and with a sobbing whimper he's gone, just like that. Looking back I see him lying crumpled and inert on the pavement.

"Sonuvawhore almost pulled me out with him." Moses grumbles, tugging the door shut. We round a bend and he watches out the back window. "See, I knew that'd make them stop." There's no sign of the patrol car behind us. "Next time they won't fuck around, not with me they won't."

We slow quickly and turn off onto the rutted road to the grove of poplars.

CHAPTER SEVEN

Brother Bell Escapes

With the boat's motor shut off the Farm is very still. A breath of wind bends the long scrubby grass in the yard, but aside from that there's no movement, no sign of anyone around.

"They must've heard the boat so where in hell are they?"

We stand on the bank of the stream with the boat hauled part way out of the water.

"Hey!" Moses shouts.

There's no answer. The log fortification at the woods edge on the hill is unmanned.

I holler: "Liz! Cavanaugh!"

"Shutup. Do you want to bring the cops down on us?"

"What do you think's happened?"

"I'm going up to take a look. Put that boat back in the water and get ready in case—" His eye catches something and he stops. Coming out of the trees beyond the barricade, stepping hesitantly and feeling ahead of him with one hand, is Cavanaugh. He trips and falls to one knee and gets up. "Is that you?" he calls.

"What in hell are you doing there? And where's that other one?"

"Liz?"

"Who else—"

"She's been knocked out. She's in the house. That man we had here, the preacher, he got away."

"He *what*?"

Cavanaugh stumbles on towards us. He says, "About an hour ago. I couldn't do anything to stop him. I told Liz not to untie him but she wouldn't listen."

"She *untied* him?"

"Yes."

"Goddammit, I'll wring her neck. Which way did he go? How'd this happen?"

Liz, Cavanaugh explains, having nothing better to do—or from some similar motive—got embroiled in a rabid argument with the preacher about religion, and on a quirk untied him so she could watch how he behaved when the spirit of the Lord got into him. Brother Bell complied, giving an exaggerated demonstration of rolling about on the floor and ranting and moaning, and after a bit of this pleaded that he was hungry. Liz took him to the kitchen, showed him the frying pan with a hardened mush of yesterday's beans in it and told him to feed out of that. It's a heavy iron frying pan; instead of eating Brother Bell picked it up and cracked her over the head with it.

"I warned her, I said it was a grave mistake to untie him. I was in the kitchen when it happened, I heard her say there were beans in the frying pan and he said 'Which frying pan?' and she said, '*That* frying pan, you stupid thing,' and he said, 'Oh,' and then in a moment I heard this sound—*bong!*—a dull ringing sound and there were some other noises and I heard the door open and someone running off and then it was absolutely quiet. I found Liz on the floor out cold. The frying pan was there beside her and there were beans all over the place and the shotgun was lying there too so he didn't take that. I thought she was dead at first, but then I felt her heart and it was still beating, thank heavens. I managed to get the poor thing wrapped in a sleeping bag, I knew it was important to keep her warm in case of shock, and I undid her buttons so she could breathe more easily and massaged her wrists and no end of things to revive her. She did regain consciousness partially, oh it was awful, moaning and crying. I was keeping watch over her when I heard a boat and then I thought I'd better hide in the woods, I didn't know which boat it was. I couldn't do anything more to help Liz, they'd only capture both of us if it were an enemy patrol."

"We better do something quick. An hour ago, eh?"

"About that."

"He'll be long gone by now," I say.

"He might've got lost in the woods. We brought him here blindfolded, remember, so he don't know where he is."

"Which way did he go?" I ask Cavanaugh.

"Mercy, I don't know. It sounded like he went over that way, across the orchard. But he might have gone anywhere after that."

We reach the house and Moses says, "We'll take a quick look but if we don't find him we got to move out right away. I was gonna move us out after dark anyway but with Bell on the loose we can't wait. We coulda used that sonuvabitch, too."

"What for?"

"Use your goddamn head. For ransom. Them pentecosters got plenty of money."

"There's Liz!" says Cavanaugh. With a hideous groan of agony Liz materializes in the doorway, looking ghastly, much worse than usual. A swelling the size of a lemon protrudes from her forehead, it's clotted with blood, and there's blood smeared on her face and tangled in her hair. Both her eyes are blackened like a raccoon's. The front of her clothes is spattered with vomit. She leans against the doorjamb and looks wildly out at us. "There he is...." She points at Cavanaugh. Her voice is weakened, it has lost a little of its shrillness. "That's the one... My head hurts. What happened to me? I was lying on the floor—I know, that little man, that preacher—Oh, it hurts. I must have been unconscious, I know that, but I could feel him, that filthy ghoul—" She continues to point at Cavanaugh—"I might have been dying, but I opened my eyes and he was there on the floor, his head between my legs—"

"Liz!" exclaims Cavanaugh. "Liz, how can you—how can you say such a thing? It's shocking, it's absolutely untrue, why, I helped you, I saved your life perhaps—"

"I saw him, the worm, and I was hurting so much and I had no strength to fight him, and then I could hear the boat coming, and he heard it—he looked so frightened. He got up and ran away. I saw him out the door falling down and running into things, he was so terrified, and then I was sick, I became sick, I couldn't stop myself." She looks down at the front of her shirt, then holds her head in her hands. "Oh, it hurts, my head aches."

"You surely don't believe her. Gracious! That blow on the head upset her, the poor thing doesn't know what she's saying. To suggest I would perform such a—such an act at a time like—it's unthinkable. Liz, poor dear, I don't blame you—"

"Don't talk to me, don't say my name! Oh my head...."

Moses snaps at her impatiently, "Take an aspirin. C'mon, we got no time to fuck around with these crazy bastards." As we set off Moses says to Liz, "You're lucky you're feeling so bad 'cause if you were in better shape I'd kick your goddamn head clean off. And if you ever untie a prisoner again I will."

Back of the house there's an old apple orchard of a dozen trees laden at this time of year with small green crab apples. The grass and weeds around the trees grow as high as our waists. Beyond the orchard there's a logging road, for years unused except by hunters, and moss and small plants and flowers grow over it. When you cross the orchard you come to this road, it runs along the edge of the open area and disappears at both ends into a forest of evergreens.

"Now, LeBlanc, you know this path a bit, so go along that way and watch your step, and if you find him in one of the holes stay there and keep an eye on him till we come."

LeBlanc moves off to our left and I go with Moses in the other direction. "Keep behind me," he says, "and walk where I walk."

The implication of his words is soon evident: in a few minutes we come upon an open pit across the width of the path. It's one of the traps Moses prepared and which Liz warned me about. Brother Bell however had no such warning, and so, about an hour before, rushing headlong he experienced the sensation of the earth suddenly disappearing from beneath him—and plunging downward he landed with a splash and a jolt to his legs that almost drove them through his stomach.

We gaze at him now standing at the bottom of a pit ten feet deep, up to his thighs in brown water and covered with mud and soggy leaves. His futile attempts to scale the walls of the pit have left him panting heavily. His little eyes sizzle with wrath. He cries up at us:

"You get me out of this hole, you savages, look at the state of my clothes! Have you any idea what this suit cost? By the living Christ you'll pay for all this—"

"Yeah?" To me Moses says, "Get the shovel and we'll fill this hole in."

"Hold it, brother. Now one minute—you're not going to bury me alive. Praise Jesus, brother, you're not going to do that."

"Why not? After what you done, belting that girl over the head with a frying pan. We can't put up with that kind of thing. You might've killed her."

"Listen to me, brother, it was an accident. I mean, you see—listen, brother, the Bible says a foolish woman is clamorous, she is simple and knoweth nothing, for a continual dropping on a rainy day and a contentious woman are alike—help me out of here, friends—I didn't want to harm the girl but she taunted me, I asked for some food and she offered me leftover beans that weren't fit for a pig, and the manner in which she stared at me, I tell you the Bible says eat thou not the bread of one that hath an evil eye, neither desire her daintiments. She made me nervous holding that gun on me, I was afraid for my life. God took my hand and—anyone would have done the same, you understand, my friends. Get me out of here, will you?"

"The evil eye, eh? Yeah, she's got those evil eyes all right, you want to see them now, Brother, blacker than a bear's arse, that's what you done to her."

"Listen to me, brothers, I'm soaked to the skin. I could have broken my legs, I could have drowned. The earth is indeed given into the hands of the wicked. What is this all about? What have I done to any of you? Why have you set out to torture me? You've taken my car, you've taken my money"—Moses was not long seeing to that—"you've ruined my new suit, starved me, kept me in chains, hurled me into this pit, what more can you do? Why don't you let me go now. I can't give you anything else."

"We'll see about that." He jerks a thumb down the path. "Go get a rope so we can pull this bird up."

"Thank you, friend."

I return to the orchard and cross it, seeing no sign of LeBlanc, but I scarcely give him a thought, assuming he's still checking the traps in the other direction.

When I get back to the pit Moses takes the rope and throws one end of it to the preacher. "Okay, hold on now," he says. Brother Bell grips the ropes, his arms outstretched above his head, and Moses pulls. The fat little man rises a few inches and falls back with a splash, losing his balance and ending up sitting in the muddy water.

"Where's your goddamn strength? How're we gonna get you out of there if you can't hang on."

The preacher stands up dripping. "You'll have to find another way," he says. "You think this is a joke, you stand there laughing at me. But be warned, he that pursueth evil pursueth it to his own death. In the words of Christ—"

"Tie the rope around your neck, we'll pull you out that way."

"That's not funny, my friend."

"Tie it around that big gut of yours."

Eventually the preacher secures the rope under his armpits and I help Moses pull him up. He sits on the ground out of breath.

"That rope hurt, praise God," he says, untying it.

As we set off for the Farm, the preacher in front of us, Moses lets his incomparable sense of humour get the better of him. With a loutish smirk he steps up behind Brother Bell and delivers him a terrific kick in the seat of the pants that lifts him a foot off the ground and sends him sprawling. "You're moving too slow!" he growls.

From the ground a quivering outraged Brother Bell glowers up at him. There's immense passion in his voice as he says: "Oh... the fires of everlasting hell would be too good for your hide you... shit!"

We Prepare To Evacuate The Farm

There are a few hours remaining until night-fall. Our marching packs are ready but we hold off leaving. Moses decrees that we're to cross the river and to do that we'll need the cover of darkness.

When I ask him why we should take the trouble and risk of crossing the river he replies: "Only a doughnut like you wouldn't know." That's all he answers.

Persisting I say, "It'll take two trips to get us all over, with the packs and everything. There's a good chance the motor will give us away."

"Yeah? Well, they're looking for us on this side, see? And the woods is thicker over there and we're away from the highway. Now don't bother me."

Outdoors, sitting on the bench against the house, Cavanaugh is thoughtfully petting the kitten—the same kitten Moses threatened to use as a target when supposedly instructing me on the use of the rifle. I go out in the yard and sit beside him. The sun has just dropped below the trees, but its rays glow upwards and the sky is bright, a deep blue with purple and pink clouds towards the west.

"Sweet little pussy," murmurs Cavanaugh, stroking the animal's fur. The kitten purrs comfortably, eyes closed tight. "When we came here I found her in the barn," he says to me, "and I've fed her every day since. What a shame to have to leave her behind. I don't know what she'll do without me. I like a little pussy, don't you?" A tiny flood of giggles pours out of him. Then his manner becomes serious. "You don't believe that rubbish Liz was talking, I hope. My dear, I'm mortified by what she said... It goes to show what a blow on the head will do, how it can disarrange a person's mind. It's a wonder she wasn't killed. She seems better now. But her poor head must ache terribly." He drops his voice. "My dear, what happened with this Manderson fellow, the Justice Minister? I asked Moses but he wouldn't tell me."

In a few words I explain to him why we returned without our prisoner. He shakes his head slowly.

"My my my. But that's awful. Do you think it was necessary?" He looks this way and that and bends closer. "Please don't repeat this but for some time now I've had misgivings about Moses. As a theorist primarily—yes, as the philosopher in our midst so to speak, normally I don't interfere with the executive in the field—but my dear, even a man of action needs some thinking power, it's quite essential if he's to lead a major mission as that one was. If Moses had only used his head, or more to the point, if he had a head to use, we'd be in possession of our man now. There's no need for blundering and foolish mistakes. And this business of dragging Brother Bell along—what do you think of that? I totally disagree with it. Does he think we're going to get our demands for Brother Bell? My dear, he may be a minister in his own right but he's no Justice Minister, he's no Arthur Manderson. And the man's dangerous. Look what he did to Liz, and her armed at the time, too. Do you have any idea where we're going when it gets dark?"

"Vaguely," I tell him. "Across the river for a start."

"I wish we'd get started. There must be hundreds of police looking for us, not to mention the military."

"Get in here, you two, don't you hear that helicopter!"

Moses slams the door after us and out the kitchen window we watch a helicopter pass low overhead. The huge blades stutter loudly as it skirts the treetops and disappears towards the river.

"That's why we got to wait till dark," says Moses.

"Do you think they saw the boat?" says Cavanaugh. "Is it well concealed?"

Nobody says anything for a moment.

"They might've seen it but it don't mean nothing. There's boats all over this river. What they're looking for is guys in a car or on foot."

But he doesn't sound entirely convinced. He adds, "Anyways it won't be long till dark."

The kitchen floor is mounded with our packsacks, we've divided amongst us provisions, utensils, sleeping bags, ammunition, maps, ponchos. Along with the packs we'll be carrying our weapons. Brother Bell is with us in the kitchen roped to a chair, wet and muddy but less hungry, having shared ravenously in our meal of canned spaghetti, cheese and sea biscuits.

Cavanaugh Plots

I feel Cavanaugh's fingers on my elbow. "My dear, is Moses still outside?" He has a quiet conspiratorial tone to his voice.

"Yes." He's prowling around the Farm on the lookout for trouble. I'm left to guard Brother Bell, in the event—Moses loudly declared—Liz should decide to untie him again. She's sitting now by the window holding her head in both hands.

Cavanaugh says something but he speaks so softly I can't make out his words. "What?" I ask.

"I say, I think something had better be done about him, the man's not fit for command. You never know what he's going to do next, and I'm not so sure he knows himself. He refuses to tell me anything. I'm grateful you're on my side in this, you've seen what he's like. I'm afraid he'll bring us all to disaster."

"What do you want to do?"

"I don't know for certain... not yet. I may be forced to assume a more active role, I may have to get right in there and personally see that things get done properly. I don't mean... not necessarily take command mind you, I mean not openly, but... in a sense effectively. Someone has to do something. I'm going to try and influence matters with greater force than I have in the past. Otherwise the outcome may be tragic. Decisions have to be made, my dear, action has to be taken, we can't permit ourselves to drift along under his haphazard direction. I plan to look out for us personally. We might try just ignoring the man. If he doesn't like it, well, let him go his own way. I know Liz will be with us. We can free the Chief. He'd be free by now if—is that him coming?"

"That's him."

"Remember. Don't let him order us around. If he says do something we must consider first, and if his proposal is not sound we'll think of something better, and do that."

Moses comes in and says, "There's a boat on the river, get your packs on and move up to the barricade. It might go by but we're taking no chances."

"Oh, dear me." Cavanaugh jumps up. "Where's my pack? Help me on with it. Hurry, please, there may not be time to lose."

I assist him into his gear while Moses unties Brother Bell. There's a pack prepared for him too which Moses throws on him; then he knots a piece of rope around the preacher's neck and holds the free end in his hand so that he has him on a leash. Liz meanwhile gets abstractedly into her pack and goes outside.

"What about LeBlanc?" I say. "What about him?"

"Where is he?" It's the first time anyone has mentioned his absence.

"How do I know? He shoulda been here long ago."

"Maybe he fell into one of the pits."

"It wouldn't surprise me. That crazy frog don't know where he's going half the time."

"Somebody ought to look for him."

"I told you there's a boat coming, so get out there, we got no time to fuck around. We'll look for him later."

Going out the door I notice Cavanaugh making his way towards the rampart. He appears to be coming from the direction of the barn, scuttling along like a long-legged beetle with his pack on his back and a package in his hand.

In a moment we are all behind cover. It is twilight and I place my pack on the ground beside me and point the shotgun towards the bend in the stream.

The Defence Of The Farm

Somewhere on the river, not far off, the boat's motor gurgles throatily. I release the safety catch on the shotgun. Bony fingers are tugging at my sleeve. I shake my arm away, too intent to give attention to Cavanaugh. I hear him whispering, "Do you see them yet? Are they coming in? Tell me when they're below us—be sure and tell me—"

Moses speaks through his teeth to Liz and me. We are to his right and Cavanaugh is squatting behind me; the preacher is sitting on the ground with his back to the wall. "Don't open fire before I do. If they land here we'll let them have it, but wait till you hear me first."

"It sounds like a big boat." It sounds like a diesel motor. "Do you think they can come up here?"

"You don't know how big it is. Keep your mouth shut. If they don't come in they can land men out there on the river bank."

But they come in all right.

Off the mouth of the stream the powerful engine cuts back and in the near darkness the sound draws closer and closer; there's no mistaking where it's going. With straining eyes I see the nose of the boat creep cautiously into view around the bend.

"What is it? Are they there?"

"Shh. Be quiet."

There are three uniformed men standing shoulder to shoulder towards the bow. It's a smaller boat than it sounded, a diesel-powered speedboat without cabin, and there's a flag fluttering on the stern. Two of the men are holding rifles. I follow their hovering advance keeping the centre man sighted down the twin barrels of the shotgun.

"How many are there?"

"Three. Shh." Cavanaugh and his foolish talk of wresting command from Moses... and his casual assumption that he's our theorist, our philosopher... ludicrous. "They'll hear you." But he's faded away from behind me. The boat reverses its engine and comes to a dead stop, idling in the stream's narrow channel, and the men are pointing towards shore at our boat and at the farm buildings. In the night shadows at the border of the woods we are well obscured. The men are talking on the boat, their words are drowned by the gurgling engine; but I know their dilemma, I can easily imagine what's troubling them. If we're here they don't dare land or turn their searchlight on for fear we'll open fire—they are standing in the open and we're concealed. But if we're not here... how will they know without investigating? The sweat is running down my forehead and into my eyes. I blink to clear my vision. "They'll have to leave," I think, "go for help from the land side." I hear a sound behind me, a slight scratching, a faint hissing. Out of the corner of my eye I glimpse Cavanaugh. Then I look quickly around at him. He's hopping about making little steps like a shotputter, I see his strange gangly figure with jerky elbows and knees, he's dancing like a marionette; he rears back and his arm shoots forward and flying through the air goes something that looks like a large firecracker with wick trailing sparks. "Heads down everyone!" he cries. And he himself plunges to the earth behind the barricade. He squeals again. "Down! Dynamite!" Moses curses and we all drop flat behind the log wall. The patrol boat is a hundred yards away and Cavanaugh's toss travels at the most a third that distance, closer to us than them, and so far off line that it hits the side of the barn—where the supply of stolen dynamite is stored. When the stick explodes so does the entire barn. WHUMP! WHUMP! BOOM! The ground shudders amid a brilliant flash illuminating a mass of flying shingles and boards and great clods of earth. "Praise the Lord!" I hardly hear the preacher's oath, my head is suddenly filled with cotton wool. And then there's a ringing silence and nobody moves. I rise slowly to my knees. The barricade thankfully is still more or less standing—or that would have been the end of us —several of the thick logs are blown awry but the mass of it remains. Through the settling dust and the last faint light of evening I make out the patrol boat floating upside down in the stream; and on the far side the three officials are in the process of dragging themselves up on the bank. I watch as they hobble into the bushes and disappear.

On his feet Moses brushes earth out of his hair, staring grimly at Cavanaugh who is still hugging the ground. I half-expect him to point his rifle at Cavanaugh and shoot him right then and there. But he says merely: "Get your packs on and let's get moving. Someone might've heard that sound."

Cavanaugh stands up and looks dimly around. "Ooh, that was loud. Did I get them?"

"My head!" complains Liz. "It's worse now. And they got away too! I saw them."

"They got away?" But Cavanaugh doesn't seem too dismayed. "Oh dear. Well, is everyone all right?"

He has with him in a paper bag four other sticks of dynamite that he took from the barn, or what used to be the barn (in its place is a sizable crater). Before we move off Moses says, "You can leave those here. If I catch you with another stick of that stuff I'll shove it up your arse and light it."

"Anyway, they'll think now that we have heavy artillery."

"Hah! Heavy artillery."

There's no question of crossing the river now, there's no time for it. Following Moses' lead we march single file along the emergency escape path, the route that leads to the rope bridge Liz showed me two days ago.

CHAPTER EIGHT

Race Against Encirclement

It was bad enough crossing the bridge in daylight.

Moses tells me to cross first, the idea being for me to cover the others as they follow. But they are impatient, they call after me to move faster, and even before I reach the other side black shapes are strung out along the bridge behind me. Increasingly the ropes sway and toss, then begin to buck furiously, and burdened with pack and shotgun I narrowly manage to reach the other side. As I step down there's a cry from behind me, a helpless "Oh oh!" followed by an enormous splash. Cavanaugh's sudden departure gives an added jolt to the ropes and the preacher gets flung off after him. Another big splash.

Moses bellows across at me: "Get in there and get him! Get that pentecoster. Liz, get back." The bridge continues to pitch wildly.

"I *am* back. I'm waiting until you all get across, or *fall in*. I knew this would happen so I waited! Ha ha!" She shrieks with delight and triumph.

"Don't let that pentecoster get away!"

Cavanaugh and Brother Bell are making a great commotion in the stream, splashing and sputtering and trying to right themselves in the running current. Dropping my pack I wade in up to my thighs and fish them out, then hold the preacher's leash until Moses and Liz are safely over. (I know for the rest of the night, or however long we march, my boots will squish and my legs chafe from the wet pants, but for Cavanaugh and Brother Bell—not only their clothes but their packs are sodden and heavy, and when we make camp their sleeping bags will certainly still be wet!)

With the bridge released and hauled in and concealed in the bushes we plunge headlong into the black wall of spruce and fir trees and push forward with all the haste we can make. From the start the going is clumsy and laborious, something like wading through deep water, and it's no time at all before I hear Cavanaugh in front of me wheezing and gasping loudly for breath. I continually blunder into him and have to prod him forward. We have no time, nor in fact any need (since we were able to prepare our packs beforehand) to stop at the cache of emergency supplies; until we cross the highway we are vulnerable to encirclement. With the river to one side and the highway to the other we are in a stretch of forest and fields less than half a mile across.

After the explosion at the Farm and the turmoil with the rope bridge we make no attempt to be quiet; in our haste we sound like a squadron of tanks plowing through the trees. The night has blackened further, heavy clouds have come over and there are only a few stars showing, and these will soon be gone.

I bang into Cavanaugh again; Moses without warning has halted sharply at the edge of the roadside ditch. Now, he says quietly, we must be very stealthy. Down the highway the lights of a car approach and we crouch low while it roars past. When its tail lights vanish Moses whispers that I am to go first, as at the bridge, and cover them when they follow. "Keep low and don't make no noise," he warns.

I creep down the broad ditch and up the other side and jog lightly over the asphalt and into the opposite ditch. There I wait, shotgun ready. For a while there is nothing. Then a sliding and clattering and grunting from across the road and feet trotting and two shapes join me in the ditch. More noises, not quite so pronounced, and a hesitant shadow is before us, moving slowly, and a whisper, "Where are you?"

"Here, you knobhead! We can't see no better'n you."

Cavanaugh slides into the ditch beside us. Another flash of lights appears down the road and we withdraw up the back of the ditch and into the trees. When the car is past Liz comes over and wasting no time we move off. It is rising ground for some distance, tangled rugged going but we rush forward at a frantic pace until we've put a mile or so behind us, and then we pause for a rest. Cavanaugh slumps down in front of me. Panting and gasping he suggests, between breaths, that this would be a good place to set up camp. But in a few minutes we are on our way again.

The March Through The Night

It's as black as the depths of a coal mine. "Join hands with Jesus—share in his boundless love—" Brother Bell up ahead begins singing—"His blood washes us whiter than snow—back to the word of God—We've heard the everlasting—" There's a yelp and the singing ceases. "Praise Jesus, brother, you're going to choke me to death—"

"Cut the howling."

"That was a hymn, brother, I have to do something—to lift my spirits up—God knows I can hardly keep on my feet—"

"Shut your trap."

I hear their voices above our crashing through the bush but I can't see them. In fact I can see absolutely nothing, not Cavanaugh in front of me, not the trees, the ground, the starless sky, not even my hand held an inch from my face. Moses, tugging the preacher along behind him, forges ahead and we follow by sounds alone; and there is no shortage of sounds to follow. We fend off an advancing forest, trip over roots and stumble into gullies, and flounder through tangled underbrush. A herd of buffalo wouldn't make more noise. Springy branches snap into our faces and pointed twigs stab us like darts; over one stretch we splash through swampland up to our knees, stagger helplessly into each other, curses fill the air, growls to shutup, laments of exhaustion. Anyone pursuing would have to be deaf not to hear us.

§

Once Moses calls, "Halt," and Liz repeats, "Halt," and Cavanaugh whispers over his shoulder, "Halt," and we all halt. I want to take my pack off, the straps are biting into my shoulders and my body aches from the backward tug of the weight. But to take it off and put it on again is too much trouble so I stand there and bear it like a mule. A flashlight flicks on aimed at the ground, a small circle of light. By it I see a folded map and a compass. Then the light goes out. "Let's go." The army, or what sounds like one at any rate, moves off again.

§

"Stop it! Stop it!" Liz screams at the top of her lungs.

"What's going on?"

"This pervert—this filthy pig! Even *now* he

won't leave me alone! Do you know what he's doing? Do you?"

"Liz, now Liz—"

"He's feeling my behind!"

"Oh for heavens sake—"

"Youse two, goddammit, keep your mouths shut—if I hear another word out of either one—"

"He's pawing me!" In the dark her incredulous eyes must be staring wildly about her. "Every step I take I feel his slimy hands all over me!"

"Not so—no, it's not so..." Cavanaugh's words come out in tired gasps. "Gracious... falling all over the place... how can I help—help running into her?"

"Change places. And no more talking—not another word out of yez."

"What?"

"Which one are you? Here—back here." By the bodies pushing past me he is placing one of them in a new position. Liz cries indignantly. "Get your dirty paws off me! Who do you think you are?"

We are moving again with Liz bringing up the rear and Cavanaugh still in front of me, behind Brother Bell.

But that isn't the last out of her. We proceed very little further before a banshee shriek sends chills up my spine. "My head still aches!" This is followed by: "And what are we doing here? Where's that Minister of Justice? Where is he? It's your fault, Moses, you made a mess of the job. You can't do *anything* right, and you try to throw your weight around! Who are you to tell me what to do? I'd never have made an ass of myself the way you did. You lost our prisoner!"

"You're gonna get a boot in the teeth, I'm warning you."

"If it was me I'd have brought back our prisoner."

"Yeah." Still marching forward he grumbles a moment. "And untied him and let him hit you over the head with a frying pan. Shutup."

"I will not,"

"In case you don't know it there's cops looking for us, and they got ears."

"We're far enough away."

"You think so, eh? You don't know where in hell we are."

"I suppose we're lost. I knew it. You've got us lost." Before he can get his next threat out she says, "And why are we bringing this silly fat man with us? He's no use to us. That's *your idea*. Obviously! What do you expect to do with him?"

"He's already explained that," interjects Cavanaugh, breathless, but his tone patient and conciliatory, "and I think, Liz... you shouldn't talk, or at least whisper if you have to talk... we should be as quiet as possible."

"Nobody asked you!"

"Moses wants the preacher. He wants him for ransom."

"What's that, brother?"

"Ha! Ransom. Who would pay for *him*?"

"That's enough out of the lot of yez."

"Did you say ransom?" Brother Bell, puffing and panting (we are still crashing our way through the trees) intones: "The Bible... Revelations twelve... he that delivereth into captivity shall... go into captivity. I have no money, my friends... I work for the Lord—*Yow!* you'll strangle me yet praise Jesus, watch what you're doing—"

There is no more talk for a long while, and we tramp on and on. I have no conception of how much time has passed nor any notion of where we are or where we're going. Moses... I wonder if he knows himself. After a while I don't even think about it. Mostly I think it would be a good idea to stop and sleep as soon as possible.

§

Buried in the black of night an interminable plodding forward through an invisible giant brier patch, walking on rubbery cushions of blisters and finally reeling and staggering like a lot of drunks... It happens regularly, someone stumbles and crashes to the ground and lies there with eyes closed—for it's such a blessed comfort to sink into a warm sleep so drowsy and helpless—"Get up you lazy sonuvabitch!"—muscles offering passive resistance someone struggles up and lurches forward. Cavanaugh goes down and in the dark I trip over him and Liz falls on both of us; we untangle ourselves and rise and move forward again.

Moses bulls on tirelessly, ignoring the preacher's croaks of pain as he jerks repeatedly on the leash. In the few fields we come to it's possible to see vaguely black contours and shapeless masses, their identities and distances impossible to distinguish. We labour over a log fence and trudge across open ground, and there's the damp smell of plowed earth and the mud cakes on our boots. Another fence brings the smell of pine needles and spruce balsam, and the resilient arms of the evergreens push stubbornly back at us as we stubbornly force our way through them.

§

Cavanaugh is down flat on his back, arms and legs outspread; he's faintly visible as the night at last begins to wear away. He whines, "Can't get up... I can't."

"Get on your feet."

"I'm trying (gasp, pant) but... nothing happens... why not... stay here?"

"We can't. Gimme your hand."

Moses pulls him up. Dazed, rubbery-legged, Cavanaugh is moving forward again.

"It's getting light." My voice sounds as if it's in an echo chamber. It doesn't even sound like my voice. I wonder if I spoke or if it was someone else, or if I imagined a voice. I say it again. "It's getting light." It sounds the same, ghostly.

There's a grayish tint in the atmosphere.

"We're just about there." Moses' voice echoes and re-echoes in my head.

§

We drag ourselves down a narrow gravel road before turning off onto a fern-covered trail leading into the forest. Later we leave this trail and proceed a few hundred yards through the bush and come to a small clearing. In the twilight Moses has his pack off and numbly I drop mine to the ground.

"I'll take first watch," Moses says. "Don't put your stuff there—keep in amongst the trees."

"I'm *hungry*. I don't think I'll eat now. I could keep on going if I wanted, I could do it all over again!"

The wind sighs and whispers overhead. Aching, shivering in the damp chill of early morning, I edge into my sleeping bag. I have one last little thought, Cavanaugh and Brother Bell—their sleeping bags will be wet. Laughing weakly I fall dead asleep.

Morning Watch

The bridge is jumping wildly, like a giant hand has hold of it cracking it like a whip, and it's all I can do to stay on. Over there, standing on the far bank, they watch with gaping mouths. So hard to hold on and keep my grip on Manderson and keep him on the bridge too. Down below us, far below there's a heavy sea, its great waves smash against the rocks, the rocks point up at us sharp as swords. The others wait in silent disbelief, astonished that I've recovered the Minister after all but the bridge is alive and tossing me—Moses shakes me roughly. "C'mon you lazy bastard, get up. It's your watch."

"It's further across—"

"What?"

My dream clings to me, I don't know what nonsensical thing I've started to say. "Nothing." Feeling as lethargic as a wet log I lie on my back and stare dopily at a pine bough directly above. A light wind moves through it, the needles tremble delicately against a blue sky. I close my eyes again. It's very peaceful, pleasant and peaceful with the scent of the trees and their gentle soughing and the brilliance of the morning. Sleep is irresistible... to drift off...

I'm given a shake that almost dislocates my shoulder. Moses' beard-stubbled face stands over mine, his eyes squinting and shiny. "Do I have to drag you out, or what?"

"No. What time is it?"

"Nine." He leaves me and sets about preparing his sleeping bag. He rolls it out and unzips it and sitting on it removes his boots. "Wake that Liz at twelve." His voice sounds slurred, you'd almost think he was drinking; he must be very worn out, even him.

"Tell her this time if that preacher gets away I'll hang her from the nearest tree... might be up by then meself... if I'm not someone's got to take the watch and there's no one else... except blind-eyes there and a lot of good he is." With the sleeping bag wrapped around him he adds, "And you, don't you go back to sleep." Then he rolls over and in a minute is snoring mightily.

I search around for my boots and find them in the grass. They are soggy and muddy and I decide not to put them on yet. The morning is warming, the mud will dry before long. I tie the laces together and hang the boots over a branch in the sun.

Brother Bell stirs. I grip the shotgun. His eyes blink open and look at me.

"It's cold, brother," he says hoarsely. "Why don't you light a fire over here. Praise Jesus everything's wet, I'll get pneumonia."

He closes his eyes again. He's lying in the shade and thinking the sun will help dry him I go over and grasp his sleeping bag by the foot and drag him out in the open. Startled he sits up.

"You'll be warmer in the sun," I say. He looks thoughtfully at me for a moment and says, "Thank you, my son. Praise the Lord!" Then he dozes off.

CHAPTER NINE

Brother Bell Gets An Assignment

In the afternoon Moses makes Brother Bell dig a latrine. The latrine is unnecessary, we are to be there only till nightfall and it's a simple matter to slip behind a tree; but Brother Bell labours most of the afternoon digging it and not long after he's finished we pack up and leave and it gets used only once, by Moses. This matter of the latrine comes up when we are eating a lunch ration of sardines and cheese and hardtack. The preacher, sitting in the grass with his leash tied to a tree, has been squirming uncomfortably for a while, sweat beaded on his face. Suddenly he says:

"Brothers and sisters, it says in the Bible, these are the words of Moses of the Holy Bible, Deuteronomy twenty-three, and Moses said thou shalt have a place also without the camp whither thou shalt go forth abroad, and thou shalt have a paddle upon thy weapon and it shall be when thou wilt ease thyself abroad thou shalt dig therewith and shalt turn back that which cometh from thee, for the Lord thy God walketh in the midst of thy camp to deliver thee. Friends ..."

Our Moses has his mouth stuffed full of food and half-intelligibly he says, "What're you talking about?"

"I have a feeling he wants to go to the bathroom," offers Cavanaugh.

"There's no bathrooms around here. Where do you think we are, in a hotel?"

"Well, you know what I mean. He must want to have a bowel movement."

"A bowel movement!" screeches Liz.

"Yeah? Is that right, Bell? You want to have a shit?"

"I don't use the term myself, but—yes, I have to, brother."

"Well, you can't."

"But I have to."

"We ain't got no latrine dug yet."

"I can go behind a bush. Praise God, I can't wait too much longer."

"You're gonna have to. We can't have you shitting all over the place, someone might walk in it."

"I can dig a little hole."

"You're damn right you can. This camp has to have a latrine or it ain't a proper camp. See that shovel? Right there on your pack, right there, you been carrying it. That's what I brought you along for, we need someone to dig the latrines for us. You don't think we're feeding you for nothing."

He unstraps a small camp shovel from Brother Bell's pack and leads the preacher by his leash to a spot at the far edge of the clearing about thirty yards away. Tying the end of the rope to a tree he says, "Okay, start digging."

"But brother, I need to relieve myself first. I've suffered from the plague of constipation for a week, and now I have to—"

"I want it dug six feet long, got that? And make it two feet wide and at least three deep. And be sure that the sides are straight 'cause if they ain't you'll be digging another one."

"But—"

"Get to work and no backtalk. If it ain't done in two hours you'll find yourself hanging by the heels from that branch up there. And if you don't think I mean it just try me."

"The Lord will smite thee, brother, the Lord will smite thee with the botch of Egypt." Moses walks away leaving him holding the tiny shovel, his face crimson with anger. "And with the hemorrhoids! And with the scales and the itch whereof thou canst not be healed!" Moses stops. The preacher quickly pushes the shovel into the earth, muttering as Moses continues on. "...smite thee with a sore botch that cannot be healed from the sole of the foot unto the top of thy head... If I do it in my pants you'll be sorry! This ground's too hard, the shovel's too small! The shovel's too small. You have no heart, my friend. I tell you—"

"Get to work you crazy bastard and no more lip."

Before long I am keeping guard over Brother Bell who is off his leash so he can reach the dimensions of the latrine with his shovel. His clothes are drenched with sweat and his chubby face glows from exertion. After each little shovelful he stops and groans and pants and wipes his forehead and says, "Praise Jesus!" and shakes his head vexedly and struggles through another shovelful. Once the sods are dug up the earth is soft enough, there are few rocks, but there are roots and these give him the devil's own time.

"That man is cruel and vicious," he says to me. "His heart's made of stone. His soul's blacker than pitch. My boy, what are you doing in the company of a man like that? It says in the Bible, Solomon chapter one, walk not thou in the way with them, refrain thy foot from their path for their feet run to evil and make haste to shed blood." He applies his foot to the shovel and scoops up a little earth and throws it aside and pauses for another breather. Over the way Moses is occupied with maps, he has a pencil and protractor and a compass laid out on a map and is making measurings of some kind. Cavanaugh, I notice, has his journal pressed against his nose and is busy writing in it. Liz is in a typical pose, sitting cross-legged on her sleeping bag in a trance, Normally the preacher's voice is hoarse and voluminous but now as he talks to me he speaks softly.

"He's a Jew, that man," he says.

I ask him why he thinks that. I have a shady spot to sit in while overseeing the shovelling, and the shotgun rests against my thighs and I have nothing to do but shoo away flies, so I see no harm in talking with our prisoner. Just so long as I'm watchful in case he tries the same trick with the shovel as he did with the frying pan.

"Look at his name. Moses. You never see a Christian with that name. And no Christian would carry on the way he does either. I tell you he's a heathen, a godless damnable heathen, he's no good at all that man. You know your Bible, my son, it was him and his kind nailed Christ Jesus to the cross and he'd do the same to any other Christian. Don't be misled, he'd do the same to you and me and think nothing of it. Upon a stranger thou shalt lend upon usury, but unto thy brother thou shalt not lend upon usury. Deuteronomy twenty-four, it tells you right in the Bible what they're like, these Jews, they stick with their own but God help you if you're not one of them. They don't accept the true Christ, they nailed our saviour on Calvary cross, and without God in their hearts what can you expect of them? Think of that, my son... The light may be dim but I see it still shines in your eye, you have the faith, it's time to nurture it, it's not too late, don't turn your back on God... That henchman of Satan is watching us—" Breaking off he digs two shovelfuls in rapid succession and then straightens and puts his hand on the small of his back. "Like Job the Lord has seen fit to try his humble servant. Young man, you have the faith I say, I know in your heart you believe, for the light of the body is in the eye, if therefore thine eye be single thy whole body shall be full of light, but if, said Jesus, and these are Jesus' own words, these are not my words but the words of Jesus who died for our sins—but if thine eye be evil thy whole body shall be full of darkness and thou shalt burn in the fire of eternal hell. Do you hear that, my son? The light shineth within you... Come back to the Bible, take God into your heart... It was a sad day when you fell in with this gang of murderers and thieves and now God asks you to repent... What can you hope to gain from a life of crime, besides the loss of your eternal soul? You may ransom me for a few dollars but mark my words that barbarian over there will keep it for himself, and if you protest he'll kill you. I know his kind. And the others are vicious as well, that girl is not in her right mind I think, and the other one, I heard his filthy tongue, a sexual pervert—and where does that leave you, a God-fearing intelligent young man, a decent young Christian who's momentarily strayed off the path of righteousness, who's left the ways of the Lord and now yearns to return! Think of your poor parents, my son. Oh on this very day somewhere they must be weeping, moaning for their lost son, but there's time, brother, it's not too late—"

"That's none of your business."

"Do they know—"

"I said it's none of your business."

"Ah yes. Brother, pardon me if I caused you pain, if I offended you, we hold our loved ones close to our hearts, yes, and your heart and soul are straining to the Lord and the Lord knoweth how to deliver the godly out of temptation and to reserve the unjust unto the day of judgment to be punished—"

He's silenced by a shout: "Hey! Get to work, pentecoster! Don't stand there leaning on your shovel! What's that fat bastard jawing about?" Moses glares over at us.

"Nothing," I call back.

"He ain't there to talk he's there to dig, so don't talk to the sonuvabitch."

"Thanks, friend," says Brother Bell, throwing more earth aside.

"Thanks for what?"

"That brute doesn't have to know about our little conversation, we have nothing in common with the likes of him, praise God." He exerts himself with the shovel for a few minutes and stops again. "Blessed Jesus it's hot!" He wipes his brow. "Whew! You wouldn't—brother, you wouldn't dig for a while, would you, I'm afraid my heart will give out."

Seeing what must be a look of astonishment on my face he says quickly, "No, I can't let you, my son, it would only get you in trouble, no, I'll keep on until I drop. Thanks for your kindness though, I won't forget it. When this is over I'll tell them there was one good man amongst them, one who took pity on a poor prisoner and aided him at every turn, one who was not like the others. No, this good man, I'll tell them, was not evil like the others and it's our Christian duty to forgive him, nay, more than that we must reward him. We must reward this good man. My son, return to God and you need fear nothing, Christ himself will see to that, you'll come to know peace and joy and happiness for if you walk in the way of Jesus all your fears and sorrows will pass away. Our saviour said, lay up for yourself treasures in heaven where neither moth nor rust dost corrupt and where thieves do not break through nor steal, for where your treasure is there will your heart be also." He digs the shovel in and with a grunt raises and empties it. "Praise the Lord! You'll go free, my son, I promise you that, I have influence in these matters, many of my brethren in Christ are men of prominence and I'll speak out for you, have no fear. This young man, I'll say, this young man saved my life, yes, my friends, he saved my life, it's to him alone I owe my liberty. While all around there were wolves who sought to devour me one lamb of the flock of God appeared and he was my deliverance. Yea, not only shall you go free, brother, but you'll be rewarded handsomely, for my flock will exult at the return of their poor shepherd and I will see to it that a collection is taken up and this will be yours, my boy, to do with as you will. It means a new start in life for you—think of it. You'll want a good job, one that pays well and with a chance for advancement: I'll see personally that you get it. You can buy yourself a lovely new car, yes, and take the young ladies out, yes, a chance to start life over again on the right foot. My son, you are truly worthy of rehabilitation. When the prodigal son returned he was forgiven, and embraced and made happy." He looks at me intently, his expression brimming with sincerity and saintliness; then he glances in the direction of Moses and says, "Well, brother, let us act soon."

"Act soon?"

"You have only to turn your gun upon the others and we are both free—free of that fiend's tyranny and free to live in the way of the Lord. You will be a hero, my boy, a hero!"

"What... what do you have in mind? Do you want me to shoot Moses?" I say, as though I'm as stupid as he takes me to be.

"God's will be done. He would shoot you quick enough."

I nod. "What about the others?"

His little eyes dart back and forth. He whispers hoarsely, "That will be easy! Once the big one is taken care of the others will be no trouble. I see his rifle over there. When you have him covered I'll get it."

I shake my head. "I've got a better idea."

"What, then? What's your plan?"

He must take me for the worst kind of simpleton. I decide to let this game go no further.

"My plan is this: you keep on digging. You don't really think I'd let you free."

"Brother—"

I shake my head. "You might as well forget about it."

He is silent for a minute, still looking at me, but now his expression hardens slightly.

"You'll regret it, my boy. This is your chance, your last chance, if you don't take it God help you. It'll go hard on you.

"I'm not a traitor."

"You're a traitor to God if you don't."

"God? I don't care. I don't know any God."

"Then you'll burn in hell."

"I don't know where that is either."

"You will, my boy, you will. When you get there."

I merely shrug my shoulders. You can't argue with a man like him; I'd have to listen to him quote the Bible to prove that the Bible is the word of God... and God exists and heaven and hell because the Bible says so, and the Bible is the word of God because it says so in the Bible.

"What do you hope to gain from this?" he says after I've kept my silence. "If you don't get killed you'll spend your life in prison. And what's it for? A few dollars if you're lucky. It's a bad bargain, friend, so think over what I've said. Listen, here's another chance, it'll be easier; when you're keeping watch and the others are asleep that's the time. You let me slip away and pretend you fell asleep. What could be easier? No one will get hurt. And I'll keep all my promises to you. I swear I will, I swear by the blood of Christ. Do that tonight, or tomorrow, whenever it's your watch. It's the last chance you'll get. Otherwise you'll be in real trouble, mark my words."

I shake my head. I have to suppress a smile; I must play my role very well if he thinks I'm that much of a gullible fool.

"You needn't decide now, give it some thought. In the meantime I'll pray for your soul. Say your prayers tonight and see what happens, let God come into your heart."

"Is that Bible thumper still yapping? I told you not to talk to him. What's he talking 'about?"

"He wants me to let him go," I shout back.

The preacher hisses: "You little rat!"

"He does, eh? Well, if he opens his mouth again ram the shovel in it. I'm gonna be over there in a few minutes and I want to see that latrine all dug. Or else."

Through his teeth the preacher says, "You treacherous whelp, I'll see that you get what's coming to you before this is over." Angrily he thrusts his shovel into the earth and this time labours at the latrine with scarcely a pause, muttering under his breath and backing at roots in the soil, and I hear him say, "blisters... hands covered with blisters"... grumble, grumble... but he works steadily and says no more to me about escaping.

§

"What? You ain't finished yet?" Moses says.

"I'm trying, brother, this is killing me. Look at my hands."

His pink little hands are swollen with mounds of blisters. "I can hardly hold the shovel."

"If you'd done an honest day's work in your life you wouldn't be such a weakling."

"I do my work, brother, I toil for the Lord, I'm not a ditch digger, I'm not used to this."

"Well, you will be when you're finished."

"It's deep enough now, praise God."

"It ain't half deep enough. And how come you ain't got a seat put up. Where's a man supposed to sit?"

"You didn't say anything about a seat."

"You drive two stakes in, one here and one here, see, and then you put a pole across, you can tie it on with rope. We got no nails. Do that when you're finished digging."

"We don't need a seat, brother."

"Nobody asked for your opinion. Once that's done you can have your shit."

"It's no good now, I'm constipated again. It's your fault for making me wait—"

"Out of me way."

Pushing the preacher aside Moses lowers his pants, straddles the pit, and in front of us all defecates noisily. The preacher looks on aghast. In the midst of this gross performance Liz comes to life momentarily and lets out an unearthly shriek. "Pig! Pig!"

"Ah, that's better," says Moses, pulling up his pants. "Now keep digging till it's another two feet deep." Then he saunters away, saying over his shoulder, "And what I said about hanging you by the heels still stands. You got another hour to get'er dug."

Cavanaugh Defends His Leadership

Cavanaugh sits himself wearily down beside me in the shade; he looks grimy and haggard. He has his notebook and pencil with him. "My dear—that is you, isn't it? I ache all over, how do you feel?"

"Tired and sore," I reply.

"Madness," he says, "utter madness marching all night like that. Where is he?"

"Who? Moses?"

"Yes."

"Over there. He's studying maps."

"Can he hear me?"

"No."

"I'll speak quietly anyway. It was revenge, that's what it was. Revenge pure and simple. I've got it written down—" tapping his notebook—"the whole story to date. My dear, by these words the history of our struggle will be known. I'm pulling no punches. Can that preacher hear me?"

I've situated myself further from the latrine now, at a point where I can keep an eye on Brother

Bell but not have to listen to him.

"No, he's too busy shoveling."

"Good. I don't have to ask about Liz, I was just over there. She won't talk to me today, she acts strange, very silent and remote. I spoke to her but she wouldn't answer." He leans closer to me and says emphatically: "Revenge!" Letting that sink in, he goes on: "He did it to pay me back, to try and break my spirit, he's afraid now that I've usurped his position, that I've in effect assumed command. I said I would, my dear, you'll recall my telling you we couldn't rely on Moses. You'll recall I promised that the first time serious action was needed I'd have to take matters into my own hands. Well, you saw for yourself. Can't you picture our fate if I hadn't used dynamite? Moses would have begun shooting and those men would have shot back and we'd have been pinned down and while we were exchanging gunfire their reinforcements would have arrived and surrounded us. I foresaw this. I knew I had to intervene and so I conceived the tactic I used. As you witnessed it was a total success. I drove the enemy off, nobody was injured and as a result we made good our escape. Just consider: if there had been a gun battle one of us might have been badly wounded or even killed, and even if we'd successfully killed the men in the boat it wasn't necessary, indeed it would have been a mistake. When you perform unnecessary killing, my dear, you stand to lose popular support. Unfortunately Moses fails to understand the simplest things. You know what he's like, you can't tell him anything." After a pause he says, "Honestly now, wouldn't you think he'd appreciate my achievement? I was able to make victory possible in our first skirmish—which, by the way my dear, I've got written down here in my notes; I've recorded it as 'The Glorious Farm Defence'—but to what effect? His reaction is bitter jealousy, and he's lost no time in getting back at me. He appears to be more concerned with his own position than the success of our cause. Oh, that gruelling march last night wasn't necessary at all, not after we were safely across the highway. Once we were a mile or two into dense forest nobody could find us. All we had to do was halt and rest for the night and resume our march at daybreak. If we had we'd be further along than we are now. But no. Instead we made the most awful commotion and gave our bodies a severe battering, and though it's true we've reached this far it was only by luck; and now we're badly weakened physically, which could prove dangerous in the event of another attack. No, my dear, he did it to try and break me. He was desperate to regain his hold on the leadership. Mind you I don't care a jot if he calls himself our commander, titles mean nothing to me, but if he'd let someone with intelligence make the decisions we'd be far better off. Don't you agree?"

"I think... you'll find things work out... in the long run." It's impossible for me to say more, though truthfully I would like to reassure the poor misguided fellow.

"Yes? I'm not sure what you mean. But I hope so. I hate to sound pessimistic about things but with Moses, you know..."

After a bit he says, hesitantly, "By the way, have you seen that, er, French fellow around?"

"You mean LeBlanc? No, LeBlanc's not with us anymore."

"He's not? Oh." He considers this a moment. "It's so hard to keep track of everyone. Where do you suppose he is?"

I explain about LeBlanc going with us to look for the preacher and not returning.

"But didn't anyone go look for him?"

"No. I mentioned it to Moses but he wasn't interested."

"That's terrible. The poor little fellow, he probably fell into one of those pits. He could starve to death."

"Perhaps. But I doubt it. The police will be all over that area today. If he's in a pit and he hollers someone will likely find him."

"I guess so. Oh well. But there it is, Moses again. Is he just irresponsible or does he do these things on purpose? Sometimes I wonder ....

Moses Gives A Briefing

It is early evening before Brother Bell climbs feebly out of the latrine and staggers a few feet and sprawls himself in the grass. He lies there panting like a fish out of water, holding his raw blistered hands before his eyes and gazing sorrowfully at them.

"So you're finished, are you?" says Moses. "It's about time, goddammit. You're an awful slow man with a shovel. Okay—" he raises his voice—"the rest of you characters listen—get over here—I'm gonna give yez a briefing."

When we're gathered by the latrine he holds up a map and points a big finger at it. 'Them's farm houses," he says, "and that's where we're gonna be tomorrow because tomorrow I'm making a phone call to see about getting rid of Bell here. He eats too much and he won't do no work, he's too lazy, so we got to get rid of him."

"Can he hear us?" says Cavanaugh. "Where is he now?"

"Let him hear, we got nothing to hide. I just got a few things to tell yez anyway. The first thing is, how much money we're gonna try and get—"

"That's not the first thing," interjects Liz, "the first thing is to demand the Chief's release!"

"I was gonna get to that so shutup. We tell them to let the redskin go, and then we say what ransom we want. And them's the only two things."

"Oh. What about... what about this fellow LeBlanc?" says Cavanaugh.

"What's he got to do with it?"

"If they've captured him... hadn't we better request his release too?"

"The hell with him. If he's that dumb to go and get caught they can keep him."

"But Moses—"

"Shutup. I said forget it. They ain't got him anyway. I know these frogs, what he done was sneak away home to the Baie to fish mackerel. He didn't have the guts to stick with us. Now like I was saying we don't ask for nothing else 'cause we don't have much to bargain with. We can save that other stuff for the next guy we catch."

By "that other stuff" Moses means our original list of demands which we drew up well before the abduction of the Justice Minister. Had we successfully detained him we planned to ask for the following in exchange for his release:

1) One million dollars,
2) The declaration of a National New Brunswick Day to honour the beginning of the Revolution; on this day all wage earners would receive a holiday from work with double pay.
3) An investigation into conditions at all jails, prisons, mental hospitals, reformatories, detention homes and any other conceivable institution where political prisoners are kept.

4) The publication in the press and over the radio and television of the following message:

To our friends the people of New Brunswick: The Popular Liberation Party today announces its existence.

We proudly accept responsibility for the retention of a member of the infamous provincial administration and will hold him until our demands are met in full.

If these demands are not met we cannot be held responsible for his fate. Whether he lives or dies is a decision that now rests in the hands of the gangsters who call themselves your government—but who are in fact your oppressors.

These very same felons have hounded us into captivity in the past and consistently refused to recognize our legitimate aims.

It is our intention now to bring a new and healthier order to New Brunswick.

We are dedicated to the attainment of nation status for New Brunswick and to the uplifting of all our oppressed citizens and to the achievement of a standard of life second to none in the entire world.

From an exploited and muddled provincial fiefdom New Brunswick will rise to proud and prosperous nationhood.

We recognize that all this will not happen without a struggle, for your oppressors and ours will cling stubbornly to power until it is fully and convincingly wrenched from their hands.

With the capture of the so-called Minister of

Justice we have struck our first blow for freedom.

Many more and greater blows will follow until victory is achieved.

Our forces are strong, our numbers are legion, our soldiers are everywhere; but we need your help, we must have your support, you, our friends, our brothers and sisters in revolution.

Join us then, have courage and take up the standard; let us fight side by side until victory is ours; the Popular Liberation Party will not be denied!

5) And, of course, with the Chief in their hands a further demand for his release would have been added.

"We'll have to at least give our statement," Cavanaugh says,

"Naw, we can throw away that crap for now, it don't sound so good when all we got is the pentecoster here to offer."

"Oh, certainly it will have to be reworded," Cavanaugh persists, "to account for what happened to Mr Manderson, that needs explaining to the public. But surely you don't mean—We can't just make an unqualified ransom demand—I mean, that's simply criminal kidnapping, it's what it would sound like. We need to explain our motives, otherwise nobody will know who we are."

"I'll take care of that stuff when I make the call. They'll know what it's all about."

"I can rewrite the statement—"

"Yeah, well I ain't reading a lot of horseshit like that. I'll put it in me own words."

"Oh dear."

"What's the matter?"

"Well, it ought to be formal, you know. It'll be taken more seriously that way."

"They'll take me serious, don't worry, they seen what happened to Manderson so they'll know what'll happen to Bell."

"That's not what I mean."

"Well it's what I mean, so don't argue, I know what I'm doing."

Cavanaugh does not look convinced. He says under his breath, "Dear, dear, dear" and slowly shakes his head,

"Now one thing we know," Moses resumes, "we can't get the same price for this bird as for the other one so there's no sense asking for a million dollars. I figure the most we can get is fifty thousand if we're lucky. If enough of them holy rollers cough up we might get that. We'll try anyways. There must be a lot of them simple bastards listen to him on the radio and some of them have to have money. So we'll say fifty thousand."

March To A New Camp

Every hour or so a light plane passes overhead. We are to set off at dusk. Our packs are ready and hidden in the trees at the edge of the clearing and when the plane comes over we take cover there ourselves.

A short while ago we heated beans over a small fire and ate them with hardtack and molasses and black coffee. Our rations are not excessively varied. We have cans of beans, spaghetti, herring and sardines; packages of dried soup and salt cod; cheese, coffee, sugar, salt and molasses; and hard dried-up sea biscuits. Fruit and vegetables and fresh meat, being perishables, we'll have to obtain from the wilderness, or if necessary requisition from farms—reimbursing the owners later, when the struggle is over.

At Moses' mention of our evening decampment Cavanaugh sighs heavily. He endeavours to convince Moses that we are better off where we are for another day, arguing that movement by night will attract attention because of the noise we make, not being able to see where we're going (though a lot of difference it would make in his case); furthermore, he says, it's more exhausting in the dark—so why can't we wait till morning? But all this is ignored by Moses.

"Before we leave make sure this camp is cleaned up and don't leave no traces behind," he says. Then he barks at Brother Bell, "You, pentecoster, get up off your arse and get to work. I want that latrine filled in again. Snap to it."

"Oh no ...."

In a few minutes, his protests as useless as Cavanaugh's, he is at the latrine shovelling the earth back into it.

"And cover that spot up with leaves when you're finished."

It is still light when the job is done but Moses says we'll move off anyway—he's impatient to get going, possibly a plane has already spotted our camp—so we load on our packs and in single file follow him into the bush. The hordes of black flies and mosquitos that plagued us all day continue to swarm over us as we march. They are more than a nuisance, they're an affliction, an incessant persecution; we have no repellant and it's futile to slap at them, to try and chase them away, they attack from all directions and leave no part of the body unbitten. Cavanaugh's bedraggled face is a mass of white bumps.

After the first half hour a certain rhythm sets in, a mechanical forward motion, the aching muscles become numbed and while there is still light to see by it's not so bad, aside from the flies. We pass through what looks like a stretch of petrified forest, many of the trees are dead and there's not a leaf or needle on any of them except high overhead, so that it's like being under a roof. There's a faint path through it and the ground is rolling and mossy with ferns growing out of it. Dead trees lean in all directions, cedars and spruces, some of them fallen across the path so we have to climb over them or bend to go under. You can see a long way, the trees are slender and bare, many lying on the ground, others half-fallen and leaning on each other. It's quiet and cool under the canopy of leaves and as we walk the last of the sun flares and flashes in the leaves overhead. Moses steps up the pace because we are exposed for such a long distance.

Some of the cedars are bent to the ground like bows forming perfect arches over our path. They're still alive but their crowns are pinned to the ground by dead trees that fell across them. In the wind the leaning trees scrape together loudly, as though groaning with pain.

Our path disappears and we halt while Moses checks the compass. We move on and before long the dead forest gives way to thick protective trees and we are able to slacken our pace somewhat.

§

When darkness comes it's like last night all over again, our progress is clamorous and slow—but tonight our march is of shorter duration. Around one in the morning Cavanaugh collapses for the dozenth time, and now he refuses to move. There are stars tonight and I can distinguish him buried in a bed of fir boughs and he's as inert as a corpse. I hear him sigh, "dear me... dear me..."

With Liz pushing at me from behind I try to

give him my hand to help him up, but he says feebly, "No... no, I need to rest, this is... too much for me, my dear."

"Hurry up, you're in the way! If he won't get up leave him there. He's just a bother anyway."

"Oh dear, oh dear."

Moses stomps back to where we've stopped and snarls at Cavanaugh but it has no effect. "Here, gimme your hand."

"Please... I'm too exhausted . I have to stay here a while... If I could... I'd get up... Oh dear, I've had it."

"Praise Jesus, brother, the man's right, I can't keep on either," I hear the preacher panting like a dog. "You're trying to kill us all."

"You're a bunch of lousy whiners. Alright, we'll rest here for five minutes, then we move on."

"I'm afraid I'll fall asleep," says Cavanaugh apologetically. "How... much further?"

"It ain't much further, we only got a little ways to go. We'll be far enough in another hour."

"Oh."

"So don't go to sleep."

"An hour... maybe I can do another hour."

Five minutes later Moses reaches down and takes Cavanaugh by the hand and jerks him onto his feet, almost pulling his arm out by the socket, and we are on the move again ...

Something like two hours go by before we finally stop.

The Struggle Outside

§

We are in among trees at the border of a field and we are to make camp here, Moses says, and he will take first watch again, and in the dark I grope around to find a space to set my gear and roll out my sleeping bag.

Three hours of profound sleep last but an instant. In the chill of the early morning Moses turns me out to take over as sentinel.

Liz Is Worried

It is dawn and the air is filled with the beating of wings and a raucous caw! caw! caw! caw! as a flock of crows flap around out in the field. I see them through the trees, and I see the wild flowers, clover, daisies, purple vetch, dandelions, buttercups—a bouquet the size of the field—but I am too beat to appreciate the scenery. With such a brief sleep behind me it's all I can do to keep my eyes open. There is a haze in the sky; most likely it will be a very hot day. My face feels stiff and sticky. I should get up and walk around to keep awake but I can't seem to make the effort, so I remain seated near our sleeping prisoner and rub my eyes.

It must be an hour later when Liz's voice breaks from her sleeping bag: "What are *you* doing there?" It sounds like one of the crows talking.

"What? I'm guarding Brother Bell." Her words startle me. I must have nodded off for a while.

"Where's that stupid Moses?"

"He's in the sack."

"I thought so. He always makes someone else do the dirty work." Only her staring eyes are showing above the flap of the sleeping bag.

"He stood the first watch himself," I say. I hear Moses snoring hoarsely. She makes an attempt to lower her voice.

"How do you know? Did you see him? I'll bet he was lying there drunk all the time."

"Drunk?"

"Of course. I saw him sneaking drinks. He has rum in his pack! He has two bottles of rum. I know he had them yesterday because I looked in his pack when he wasn't watching. Maybe he's drunk them by now!"

"Where'd he get the rum?"

"How should I know? He must have bought it in Fredericton and kept it hidden. He's not to be trusted. Not only is he a loutish pig but he's a drunkard too. I'm keeping my eye on him. Why do you let him push you around?"

"He doesn't push me around."

"Ha!"

I have to listen to her contemptuous laugh. There are things I would like to say but I keep silent.

"Why don't you stand up to him? He doesn't push me around. If someone else stood up to him besides me then he wouldn't be in charge very long. I can't do everything alone. Why are you afraid of him? He's only a big clown."

"I'm not afraid of him."

"He's forever telling you what to do and he makes you do all the dirty work. Do you know what you are? You're a fool. A perfect fool. Didn't you see what happened to LeBlanc?"

"What do you mean?"

"He caught him in one of his traps and left him there. And now he won't even ask for his release. Do you know why?"

I'm not so stupid as she thinks. Naturally I know why, but to myself I say, "Let her talk, out of her babblings I might learn something. I'll let her go on and put up with her insults. Besides it helps to keep me awake."

"Why?" I say aloud.

"Because he doesn't want to share the ransom money. Even a pure idiot could see that. He wants all that money for himself."

"But—"

"You think he cares about our cause? Don't make me laugh! He wants to use us so he can make a pile of money. That's his scheme. Once we get the money you just watch what happens. I hope you're prepared. You'd better be. He'll try to get rid of the rest of us. Do you hear me? He has to be stopped. You will help me stop him. When we've fixed him you can help me reorganize our group. That other one, that half-wit Cavanaugh, he's helpless as a baby. He's worse than that, he won't stop bothering me, he can think of only one thing. And he's a homosexual too. Not that you'd mind. I've watched him put his hand on your leg. He's superfluous."

I ignore her insinuation.

"But what about the Chief?" I say. "If Moses intends to do what you say, where does the Chief come in?"

"He won't come in. At least not if Moses has his way. He'll telephone our ransom demands and one of us has to be with him when he does. We have to watch him. He won't let me if he can help it but I think he'll let you, because he can shove you around. But listen when he telephones. You'll see he won't ask for the Chief."

"But he'll have to. If I'm there—"

"If he doesn't then shoot him. I'll tell him that myself, I'll tell him if the Chief isn't released and it's his fault I'll shoot him, or someone will. That will worry him. He wants all that money and it won't help him if he's dead."

"But if the Chief is freed—"

"Moses has something up his sleeve. You'll see." She's quiet for a minute. "Well, one way or another I'll look after him—the Chief will get his liberty. But the situation won't be the same. Not after he let himself be captured. Don't forget that. But he can be useful and I will free him." She stops. "Listen!"

"What?"

"Don't you hear that? Stupid!"

It is the far away drone of an airplane.

"I know, I hear it, it's a plane," I say. "But they can't see us in here, we're hidden by the trees."

"But we're moving by daylight today and they'll be searching for us with airplanes and helicopters, so we must be careful. He thinks we're far enough now, he thinks where we are now we don't have to march at night. And he's impatient to make that phone call."

"How do you know that's what he thinks?"

"He told me. After I saw him drinking he told me. We're close to a farmhouse, we can reach it in a few hours, he said, and he'll make the call and then we'll leave there quickly. He said when they find out where the call was made from we'll be far away by the time they arrive. Then we're to march all evening and into the night."

"Did he tell you how he plans to pick up the money?"

"No. I told *him* how it should be done—but he wouldn't listen and that proves I'm right about him. I told him the Chief should bring the money with him when he's released, and one of us would meet him on a lonely road and bring him into the woods where we're hidden. When we're safe away we would let our prisoner go."

"And Moses didn't like that?"

"No. He said the Chief would steal the money. He said the temptation would be too much for him."

"That's foolish."

"No. Not for him it's not. He thinks it's clever.

He tried to fool me but I know what he's doing. Just listen to him snoring. Did you ever hear anyone snore like that before? He's an animal, a stupid brute, that's what he is."

She sits bolt upright and stares hard at Moses, at the grunting and snorting hulk of Moses, and then lies down again and turns her back to me and says nothing else. Later I have to wake her to take next watch so I can catch some sleep myself, before we move off in the afternoon.

Moses Delivers His Demands

We climb a heavily wooded rise in the heat of the afternoon and when we reach the top find ourselves facing a valley on the other side. Below us a gravel road rambles along through cultivated fields and cow pastures and intervals of forest; off to the left stands the farmhouse.

"That's the one," says Moses, "and those are telephone lines along the road. I can't see if they go into the house. But someone along here's got to have a phone."

We lower our packs and catch our breath. The heat is extreme and our clothes are drenched with sweat.

"I could use a drink of water, praise Jesus," Brother Bell says, sitting in the shade and wheezing. His face looks like a steaming tomato. He has no canteen himself and I pass him mine, and when he's had a drink take one myself. The water is warm and flat.

"This heat—my word, this is worse than at night," says Cavanaugh. It has taken us about two hours to get here from the camp and Cavanaugh with his limited sight did as much stumbling and falling today as in the middle of the night.

"None of that complaining," says Moses. "We got a lot more ground to cover after this. If that place don't have no phone we'll try the one up the road. Now youse characters wait here while I go down and look after that ransom business—"

"You're not going alone!" cries Liz.

"You're goddamn right I am."

"No you're not! I told you before what'll happen, you're going to try and get away without mentioning the Chief."

"Why in Jesus would I do that?"

"You know why! You don't want him around!"

Moses scrutinizes her for a minute, and it's a very black scrutiny. But he says, "I think you're nuts but if it'll shut you up I'll take fartface here along, but just see that Bell don't get loose again. I'm gonna tie him to a tree and I want to find him there when I get back. Gimme that pistol of yours."

"Why?" She jumps back suspiciously.

"I ain't gonna go down there carrying this rifle. Smarten up. You can cover the pentecoster with the shotgun."

He stuffs the pistol in his belt and buttons his jacket over it, secures Brother Bell to a tree and says to me, "Okay, let's go."

"I don't have a gun now," I say, having given my shotgun to Liz.

"You don't need one. You don't know how to use one anyway."

I set off after him down the hill, and until we reach the first field at the base of the hill we are able to keep in the cover of the trees.

At the border of the trees we move several yards to our left to bring a barn between ourselves and the house, and then go over a twisted rail fence and head across a cow field. There are a few black and white cows in the field munching grass and as we approach they lumber out of our way and stand sullenly watching as we climb the fence at the other side and walk up the rows of a potato garden. The whole place seems tranquil; some chickens are clucking and squawking in the yard, a pig grunts in the barn, hidden hoofs stomp hollowly on wood, a cowbell clanks off in the distance—but this peacefulness is broken by the sudden appearance of two large dogs. As we reach the end of the garden they come bounding and barking around the corner of the barn and make straight for us. Moses is in front of me and the lead dog reaches him and growling and baring its teeth makes a snap at his arm—and is met by a bone-crushing whack on the head from the pistol butt. Moses it seems has his way with dogs as well as humans. With an oath he turns to the other animal but this one already is slinking away with its tail low, glancing timidly back over its shoulder. The first dog lies still on the ground. Moses returns the pistol to his belt.

"... fixed that sonuvawhore... "

As we round the barn a woman comes out a screen door and stands on the steps at the rear of the house, a cloth in her hands. Walking quickly up to her Moses whips out the pistol and shakes it at her like a finger. "Who else is in there?"

The woman is a scrawny creature of sixty. At the sight of the gun she starts trembling and fluttering and pulling nervously at the cloth. But she doesn't say anything. Moses growls his question at her again.

"Oh! Oh! I heard the—I heard the dogs—you didn't you shouldn't have... that-that-that—" She looks like she's about to faint.

"C'mon, c'mon," says Moses, "stop stuttering and answer my question."

"That—that's a gun, that's a—what did... oh no I don't think, no, oh dear. Would you, are you, well... what—no there's no one else—"

"For the love of Jesus. Do you have a phone?"

"A phone? My—I mean Mr Murdoch, I mean my husband he's out in the fields, he's he's, I think, I don't—mending fences, I think, yes Oh! I don't like guns—"

"*I said* do you have a phone?"

"Oh! A phone? A phone? Oh yes, yes, yes... we

have one—but—but we don't use it much—but sometimes, well, but you don't... yes, we have a phone—"

"That's all I want to know. Just show us where the goddamn thing is. C'mon, get inside."

With twittering fingers she opens the screen door and we follow her through a porch and into the kitchen. It is dark after the bright sunlight, the shades are drawn to keep the place cool, but it's still stifling hot. There's a wood stove burning and the smell of bread baking. The woman nervously wrings the cloth.

"Well, where is it?"

"Oh!" She jumps. "Where is—I've been making bread, the kitchen... the phone. Oh, it's... it's in this way, in the dining room. We're... we're not wealthy people, we don't have much... I hope, I mean, oh dear—"

"We ain't here to rob you. Just shutup and you'll be alright. When's your old man get back?"

"My... Oh! My husband, I don't know... I mean I think, let me think... Oh dear, I can't think, let me see... when does—what did you want to know? Oh! the phone, it's-it's... my husband get back? What time is it? Oh, I don't know..."

"Never mind. For Christsake."

The phone is on a low stand in the corner next to a glass-fronted cabinet of dishes. Most of the room is taken up by an oval table with high-backed chairs around it and everything is polished and shiny and nothing looks very much used. To me Moses says,

"Keep your eyes open. Keep a check on those windows. Wait. Ring up the paper for me first."

We are to follow our original plan of communication which Moses has seen no reason to alter. I dial the long distance operator and ask for the Saint John Telegraph-Journal. It is the largest paper in the province and the one, we've calculated, most likely to treat our activities as news—and the more publicity we get the better.

"Your number, please?"

I give the operator the old lady's number and she puts me through, while Moses stands over me breathing down my neck.

A female voice says: "Telegraph-Journal."

"Could you give me the newsroom, please."

"One moment, please."

A pause, then:

"Newsroom."

"I'd like to speak to the news editor."

"He's not in yet."

"When will he be in?"

"Half an hour or so. Can I help you?"

"Hold on a second."

I cover the receiver and pass on the information to Moses. "Will we wait?"

"Naw, we can't wait. We got to get moving. Gimme that thing—and keep an eye on the old woman."

I pass him the receiver.

"Hello. Who's that?... Never mind who I am,

you'll learn that quick enough. Are you one of them editors? I got an important message... Okay, you'll do. Now listen close, I ain't got much time and if you get this wrong there's gonna be one less go-preacher on the go. Understand?... I'm getting there, keep your shirt on. First I'm letting you know we're the ones grabbed that guy Manderson a few days ago... Yeah, right, we're the ones done it... I'll get to that in a minute. We done it to show we don't fool around. So tell the cops, you tell the cops if they bother us with this one he'll get the same treatment, so they want to lay off us... Don't interrupt me, I'll say what I'm gonna say and you pay attention... We're a revolution army, that's what we are, we got a name so write it down, we're called—what we call ourselves is the Popular Liberation Party or something, yeah, the Popular Liberation Party... I ain't the one made it up but that's what it is, and if you're wondering what happened to that pentecoster, that guy Bell, Brother Bell, we got him, we're holding him prisoner for ransom... He's that holy roller—he says he's on the radio, you must've heard... that's the one, it was his car, right, right .. . Anyhow here's what we're asking... I don't give a damn who, anyone, all them pentecosters, the government, as long as we get the money... Here's how much, write it down—and print it in your paper too, so everyone knows, and tell those sonsawhores in the government. Fifty thousand dollars. Fifty thousand and not a penny less..." He pauses and for a couple of minutes I hear the voice on the other end talking indistinctly. Then:

"That's it, yeah, we're the ones captured that Manderson guy, it was no sweat—and there ain't only me in this either, we got a lot of men and we don't fool around... Right now we got this Brother Bell character and we want fifty thousand bucks or we kill the sonuvabitch... Popular Liberation Party. What we stand for? We're revolution fighters, we're taking over this province and we're gonna make it a country, you know, like the States or England, a country like that, not just a lousy province, and we're gonna run it our way, no more bullshit from them bastards in Fredericton, we're gonna take 'er over and run things right... and we got the men to do it, right this minute we got a couple hundred fighting men and we're all army trained, the whole lot of us, and there'll be a helluva lot more of us before long, just watch—so you want to write down that they better not mess around with us' cause I can tell you we're all business.... Yeah, right, I'm the one's running her. What? I ain't gonna tell you where we are, we're hid, we're well hid so there's no point looking for us... What else was there...? The money, now I'm gonna tell you where I want the money delivered, so listen close, write this down. You ready? There's a road, okay? It's on the map, I don't know what it's called but I'll give you the place, it's a dirt road and it turns off the highway from Fredericton to St Stephen, highway three, at—take this down—latitude sixty-seven degrees thirty-two minutes—got that? Latitude sixty-seven degrees thirty-two minutes. And the longitude is forty-five degrees fifty-six minutes, forty-five degrees fifty-six minutes. If you don't understand what that means get someone who can read a map to tell you. Now, I want one guy, one unarmed guy to take the money in a car and drive all by himself east along this road for about ten miles until he gets to an old sawmill there that ain't used no more. This mill is at latitude sixty-seven degrees forty-two minutes and longitude... longitude forty-five degrees fifty-six minutes on the right side of the road travelling east. When he gets there he puts the money on the side of the road and drives away. I want it in a packsack and only tens and twenties, no big bills. Tell them that, tens and twenties, and no marked money either, brand new bills. When that guy drives away one of my men will come pick up the ransom and when he gets back to our camp we'll let the preacher go. I'll have men all over the area watching too, they'll be well hid, so don't try no funny stuff. If anything goes wrong we'll kill the prisoner... Yeah, I was getting to that. I want it delivered tomorrow at eight o'clock in the evening. Eight in the evening. Tomorrow. If it's not there by a quarter after my man will leave and that's it for Brother Bell. We'll tie him to a tree and shoot the sonuvabitch ...." There is another extended pause while the other voice talks. Moses nods saying, "Yeah, that's right, yeah, you got it right... yeah... yeah." Then: "Proof? What proof? What proof do you need, I'm telling you all this ain't I? What do you think, I made all this up or something? You'll get your proof alright if I don't see the money... No, you can't talk to him, he ain't here, he's back in the bush... We got no time for that, we ain't got time to send no note... Look, he had a red Buick, eh? and I'll tell you where they found it, it was in a field by the river not far from where I dumped out Manderson. Now, if I know that then I must be the guy that's got him, eh?... Yeah, well I don't read newspapers, where're we gonna get a newspaper away out in the woods?... We had one, sure, but the batteries run down and we didn't get no chance to buy new ones so we left the damn thing at the Farm. Enough of this bullshit, they either produce the money or else, I got no time to keep jawing with you all day—and don't go trying to trace this call because if anyone starts bothering us you know what we'll do—"

I can't hold back any longer.

"Moses—what about the Chief? *The Chief.*"

He gives me a hard look.

The buffoon! To think this is our first official communique—and this is the man who presumed to set himself up as our leader! I should never have let him go this far. I didn't need this further evidence of his incompetence.

"One other thing, I almost forgot," he's saying into the phone, "there's this big Indian, I don't know his name, I don't think he's got one, Crazy Arse, Crazy Horse, something like that—"

"Magaguadavic!"

"Magavity—it don't matter—he's probably in jail somewheres, probably Fredericton, anyway, tell them to let him go... Never mind why, just let him out of jail... a great big bastard, they woulda got him four or five days ago unless he run off somewhere by himself... They had him before, he was raising hell a few years ago in Newcastle, on the warpath about something or other, thinks there's some kinda Indian spirits telling him what to do. Anyway let him loose and send him back to the reservation... I don't know, Burnt Church I think... Yeah, he'll be happy there, he'll be able to get drunk and go trapping rabbits—and tell him I'm the one got him free... Me? I ain't gonna give you my name, have some sense... Now, I want all this printed in your paper and don't waste no time passing my message on to the government and the holy rollers, and remember, tomorrow at eight o'clock at that old mill... I got to go now, I been talking too long already." He slams the receiver down and rips the phone cord out of the wall. "That takes care of that," he says. "Kept asking questions—probably trying to trace the call. So we better hit the road."

"Yes, might as well."

"What's wrong?" He looks at me sharply.

"Nothing." To myself I say, "Nothing but you, you dumb oaf—if the Chief ever gets his freedom out of this it'll be a miracle."

"We'll tie this old whore up first," he says. "Where's some rope?"

The woman is quivering with terror, she puts her hand to her mouth and says weakly, "Rope... rope?" After listening to Moses and his threats to kill the preacher no doubt she believes he intends to hang her.

"Wait—I saw some in the porch. Get it," he says to me.

I go and fetch the rope but am far from lively about it. His phone conversation has left me dispirited; I am not in the mood for jumping to his orders. He snatches it out of my hand. "You think we got all day?"

Then he jerks the woman by the arm and flings her into a chair. "Sit down there."

A little squeak escapes her. "No ..."

"Nothing to worry about, missus, you'll be out of this before long," he says. "We just need a little time to get away without you making trouble for us."

He winds the rope around her and the chair several times and ties it and says, "There, that takes care of you, you old bag. And don't start screaming. You hear me?"

"There's no one to hear her anyway," I say.

Passing through the kitchen he stops suddenly and picks up two loaves of freshly baked bread. "What else...? Ah, we ain't got time. Here, carry one of these."

We go by the dog he clubbed and it's still lying motionless on the ground. The other dog is hanging around and when he sees us approach trots quickly behind the barn.

As we're crossing the cow pasture Moses says, "See, that's how it's done, you got to talk to them like you mean business, none of this farting around with

fancy words. You heard how I told him the directions.
That let him know we ain't no amateurs—it's how they
do it in the army. You got to be trained to use a map
like that." We reach the edge of the field and climb the
fence and start up the rise through the woods.

"One thing I might tell you," he says, munching
on the bread as we make our way up, "in case you're
wondering about the redskin. The reason I said to put
him on the reservation is he'll be safe there till we
need him. Them savages will keep him hid and when
we're straightened out with this ransom business and
got ourselves all organized we can pick him up
anytime. We got to do one thing at a time, once we get
away with the money we can put our minds to other
things. So don't go mouthing to that crazy witch up
there about the way I done things. I got good reasons.
I can't tell you everything all at once."

When we reach the top of the rise Liz springs
at us and says: "Did you make the call? Did you insist
on the Chief's release? Tell me!"

"Yeah, yeah. Shutup."

"Did he?" She turns her owlish eyes on me.

I shrug. What can I say? And why say anything
to *her*? Tomorrow—this has gone on long enough—
tomorrow is the time to make my move; there's no
question about it now.

"Yes, he did."

"He must have made a mess of it! I know! I can
tell by your expression! I'll bet he sounded like a
complete fool!" Still staring at me she adds, as though

I've been a naughty child, "I'll talk to *you* later."

"We even got some fresh bread." Moses laughs. That means he must be genuinely pleased with how he handled the call.

"You stole it!" cries Liz. "You should have paid for it! Did you pay for it?"

"Are you kidding? Now let's get a move on, we got a lot of ground to cover."

Cavanaugh Looks Ahead

We reach a hydro line and follow it keeping to the edge near the trees. It's like being on an enormous road grown over with saplings, and before us the pylons appear on successive slopes for miles like an army of robots on the march. As the sun goes down Cavanaugh walks beside me and informs me of some new plans he's conceived for himself. He says he means to go into exile.

"I'll be more effective there," he says confidentially. "I've proven I can handle life in the trenches... I've demonstrated I can hold my own with the rest of you, I've come through rather well I think as a fighting soldier... Indeed my dear I've had to give more of myself than you others, and it's taken more out of me, you can imagine how it is with my eyesight, it hasn't been—Oh! You see, you see what I mean?"

His foot strikes a root and I have to catch hold

of him to prevent him from tumbling to the ground. When he's righted he goes on:

"Dear boy, when the history of this war is written the world will know that I was there—when the fighting was the toughest, when our forces were the smallest... I was there in the thick of the battle... You've witnessed it yourself, my dear, we were comrades in arms... side by side we fought... posterity will know that... But the hour has come for me to direct my energies elsewhere... But I'll be back.... When the need arises I'll be on the front line again, I don't have to tell you that, you know my character... But abroad... abroad I can accomplish so much more..."

"Where will you go?" I ask him.

"Well, London, I think... yes, first to London, and then to the other capitals of Europe... to publicize our cause, to raise money for arms, to find loyal troops who have taken to exile in despair, and to send them home to fight... yes, dear fellow, there is so much to be done. I will begin by writing a book about our struggle, the first volume of the history of the revolution. Think of it, what that will mean, the precious funds and the sympathy and the aid this alone will bring... they'll flock to our cause, young warriors everywhere, idealistic boys and girls will be drawn to us by the thousands... by the thousands... I'll make speeches, I'll establish a supply line, an underground supply line, I'll disseminate our philosophy. Pamphlets, tracts, I'll write them tirelessly, I'll edit a newspaper in exile... these will be smuggled back to our soldiers... Oh—"

I untangle him from a young poplar that he's tripped into and point him forward again.

"It's exciting, my dear, the prospect of doing so much good work... I'll let Moses know shortly, and leave orders with him for when I'm gone... the hour has come... he has to know.... You're with me, my dear, you'll be at my right hand when I tell him... I'll need a little for expenses, not much... but we'll soon have the ransom money and it'll have to be expended on only the most vital aspects... I'm not sure how much I'll need... the absolute barest minimum, but there'll be much travel involved, and to create an underground supply system. Later I'll get money from my book, and the speeches, fund-raising speeches... it will all go into the cause, none of it for myself... what do you think, a sum of... oh, twelve thousand dollars, is that too much?... it's a starting figure, if it's considered too high we'll work it down... but perspective, priorities, what is of the greatest importance... you understand? Oh! Thank you, my dear. Yes, I've been keeping notes, I have the rough material for my book, but I can't write it on the march. You'll be in the book, dear boy, don't worry about that, you've been a faithful revolutionary and a true friend to this old soldier. You'll be there, my dear ..."

Why should I disillusion Cavanaugh? My observations have convinced me he'll have to leave us anyway, though not in such a grandiose fashion as he envisions. Twelve thousand dollars! Well, why not have him go into exile? He may not accomplish much but at least he'll be out of the way, and I won't be stumbling into him all the time. As to his book, let him write it if he wants; it can do no harm. But he has such an absurd concept of his own stature that I can't imagine its publication... that would be too much. Twelve thousand dollars he wants. I could have burst out laughing.

Cavanaugh seems quite cheered by his new idea. There is even some vigour in his step.

Before long we leave the hydro line and tramp through the bush in the waning light and when darkness is on us come to a halt.

"We spend the night here."

"Praise Jesus for that. You'll be the death of me yet, brother—"

"Shutup." Getting out of his pack he says, "An easy day's march tomorrow and we'll be at that mill, but we don't want to get too near yet so there's no point going all night, otherwise we would. I ain't stopping because of anyone's whining and crying. There's no room in this army for weaklings."

"I'm hungry!"

"Nobody's stopping you from eating. Have one of them crackers."

"I'm having more than that! It's not your food. You think you're going to be the one to collect the money, don't you? You think you'll go alone and then disappear."

"What're you talking about. Go and sit down somewhere." Moses is bent over his pack, unbuckling it.

"I won't let you—you can't be the one to go."

He looks up at her. "I ain't planning to be. Maybe I'll get you to go. Or maybe numb-nuts, I got to keep an eye on the preacher here."

For a moment she says nothing, but not for long.

"I know! I know why! You're *afraid*. You're afraid they'll set a trap and you want someone else to get caught."

"They won't set no trap. They know who they're dealing with. If they do try something they're really gonna know. Next time they won't fuck around."

"Ah! There—see? He's afraid of a trap and he wants someone else—"

"For Christsake—"

"Well? Well?

"Look, nitwit, what do you want? First you want it one way and next another. Do you want me to collect the money myself or not?"

This gives her another pause.

"You're up to something—but don't forget I'm watching you. Stupid!"

Moses just laughs at her.

Liz Warns Me

The green and yellow lights of an airplane blink through an opening in the treetops and then it disappears, the noise of its engine fading gradually away. My night watch is about half over and the few stars that were out earlier have disappeared behind black clouds. Something moves and in the dark I pick out Liz coming towards me. She sits down where I am and says:

"Tell me about the phone call—what did he say? Tell me everything!" She is trying to speak quietly for a change and her voice is a piercing hiss.

I've been going over the call in my mind, and I describe the performance Moses gave, and she says, "The pig! I told you he'd do that. But he *did* ask for the Chief? You heard him, he didn't have his finger on the receiver button?"

I didn't think of that... but I would have noticed, detected a change in his attitude, in the tone of his voice.

"I don't think so. No, he asked—it was just kind of offhand, that's all."

"They won't let him go!"

"I don't—we can't tell yet, we'll have to wait."

"You heard what I said. One of us will have to pick up the money. It's our only choice. If he went alone we'd never see him again. Well?"

"Yes," I agree, "yes, you're right."

I am almost certain Moses means for me to do the job. He believes he has me under his thumb. He must be sure I'll bring the money back—and if there's a trap, a lot he'd mind losing me. Yes, I see his plan.

"Once we have the money—if they bother to deliver it!—keep your gun handy! And don't take your eyes off him!" With that final hiss of instruction she moves away to her sleeping bag.

CHAPTER TEN

What I Must Do

Alone in the dark I come to the only conclusion possible. My decision is not easy for I'm bothered to a degree by what might happen to Cavanaugh and Brother Bell, and then there is the very real danger that I may indeed walk into a trap. There's Moses, too, he may decide to follow me at a distance, watching my every move, so I must go armed... No matter, these others, the three of them, far from needing them I am perfectly cognizant of what they are: obstacles. Obstacles on the path to victory. I've seen their worth and the war is better waged without them. Yes, and Moses in time will be dealt with, and to the extent he deserves. And Liz, if necessary. It would be best if she'd simply disappear somewhere, but knowing her there's bound to be a faction, a counter- movement, anything to put her on top, she'll try that... if she has the opportunity. But old Cavanaugh, although he's of little or no use he's harmless; I'm not a heartless person; in time I'll search him out and see that he gets his cherished place in exile until the war is won—but for now I fear they'll abandon him—it's a pity, but it can't be helped. Then too, it's possible, Moses in his wrath, if he does away with the prisoner... well, that too is unfortunate, but the struggle is everything and some who are innocent have to fall... which is not to say Brother Bell is innocent; he's on the other side all right, but it can serve no good purpose to kill him; on the contrary it would appear that we went back on our word... but I have to chance these things. Moses may stop and think in time—a message left at the mill, tell them the ransom money was paid and collected, explain briefly my decision, sign it finally: Commander-in-Chief. It should occur to Moses, his mind should think this way: "So they paid off, so the racket works, it's not a case of them not coming through with the money. Okay, I'll try again, only this time I'll pick up the money myself. I shoulda known that so-and-so was more than he pretended to be. To think all this time...." However, that's getting ahead, he'll feel the full effect later... Yes, in that case, he can't help but see the implication, he'll have to release the preacher if he's to try again. But he must be restrained, Moses, before he kidnaps someone else. If he continues to act in our name it will be no time at all before we're confused with common gangsters in the minds of the people— Moses must be dealt with—only not now, for the time being I need him to find the mill... With fifty thousand dollars and the Chief at my side (my next move: to make for the Burnt Church Reserve) and insurrection swelling throughout the countryside, in the villages and towns and cities, with an iron central command, there is hope, much hope, at last.

§

The dawn is gray, the sky heavily clouded over. I wake Liz to take over the watch. Her head feels better, she says sharply, when I inquire. She still looks like the wrath of God.

Moses Reveals His Strategy

At mid-morning I'm awakened by Liz's cackling and shrieking—it's noise enough to wake the dead.

"Listen to something funny! *Funny, funny*!"

"For the love of Jesus, sister—"

She is pointing a finger at Brother Bell and shrieking and squealing with hilarity.

"This stupid silly person wants me to run away with him!"

"Sister—"

"He said he's in love with me—and we should sneak away together! You should have heard him—Money! A new car! A big house! Servants! A summer home! An expensive new wardrobe! A trip to Europe! Ha ha!"

Brother Bell's face is more flushed than ever. His little eyes flash with malice. Raising himself up and summoning his most impressive voice he says: "My friends, don't be deceived by this Jezebel. She is lying. I say she is lying. She tried, oh she tried to tempt me with the pleasures of the flesh but I stood firm in the Lord and would not be tempted—O harlot, hear the word of the Lord! Thou art lewd and abominable saith the Lord—lewd and abominable! She hath committed fornication with the Egyptians and played the whore with the Assyrians—"

"That's not true! I did not!" Liz has stopped her cackling. "I wouldn't go near an ugly slob like you—you disgust me—you were trying to *escape* and you thought you could fool me but even a child could see through your simple tricks. And don't call me a whore or you'll be sorry—I'll cut your stupid—your silly penis off! I will!"

"Oh my, oh dear me," says Cavanaugh.

"Oh no, sister, that wouldn't do—I was making a joke—for it says in the Bible he that is wounded in the stones or has his privy member cut off shall not enter the congregation of the Lord. Jesus said from out of the hearts of men proceed evil thoughts, adulteries, fornications, murders, thefts, covetousness, wickedness, deceit, lasciviousness, an evil eye, blasphemy, pride, foolishness—all these evil things come from within and defile the man. Brothers and sisters, the holy Bible says—"

"And he says you're a Jew, Moses. Are you a Jew?"

"I ain't no fucking Jew. And I ain't no pente-coster either."

"What are you?"

"I ain't nothing."

She screams with laughter.

"Knock it off. Are you crazy or something? Get your stuff ready. We're pulling out soon."

When our packs are set to go, he says:

"We're crossing quite a lot of farmland today so keep your eyes and ears open. Late this afternoon we'll be a mile or so up the road from the mill and we'll keep about a mile in the bush. When we get there I don't want to hear none of this screeching and arguing because you can't tell, they might try to get smart and be out looking for us. In fact I don't want no talking on the way either, while we're moving. If you got to say something real bad whisper it and whisper it to me. Are there any questions before we go and I don't mean dumb questions? Okay—"

"What do we do *after* we've got the money? That is presuming we *get* it. When we've let this thing free—then what do we do? We have to have some form of plan, you know. Did you ever think of that, Moses? When we've given up our prisoner they'll be looking for us, they'll have an entire army out *searching* for us! Where do we go?"

"I got 'er thought out. You don't need to worry about it."

"Yes I do. You aren't the only one here."

"Well, I'll tell yez. And once I tell yez stop asking questions. Once we got the ransom it'll be near dark, so by the time we loose Bell—if I don't shoot him instead—it'll be night and we'll have good cover. Then we march like hell and we keep on every night till we come to Saint John. We'll hide out there a couple of days and get some good guns and a good fast car—and then we go to Fredericton again and grab another one of them politicians. Only this time we ain't gonna lose him, we won't have that frog to fuck things up—if he woulda drove that car right we'd of been away. This time I'm gonna figure out a better plan. We can get a million bucks for a politician—that's what we was planning on. This fifty thousand's only pocket money, something to finance bigger stuff."

"Well!"

"There now. I told yez I had 'er figured."

"Dear me," mutters Cavanaugh. I can see he's thinking about his money for exile.

"What's eating you?"

"That sounds rather dangerous... there are, uh, priorities, you might say... but of course I'm all for it... except... however, well, we'll talk it over in Saint John, if we reach there. That's—er—a long way."

"Yeah? You don't have to come if you don't want to—you four-eyed fucker—and I'll tell you something else, I'm getting sick and tired of dragging your useless carcass around. I don't want to hear no more complaints out of you and you'd better not slow us down. I don't know what you're doing in this outfit anyway, you're no more good than a tit on a nun, always whining and stumbling around and getting in the way."

"Oh dear. Well, in Saint John—"

"Yeah, in Saint John, when we get there you're—anyway, the hell with this, we got to get moving."

After her exclamation Liz, I notice, says nothing and there's a peculiarly pensive look on her face.

Eyes Of The Enemy

"We're not going across here, are we? It's all open. What if a plane flies over?"

"Nothing to worry about."

We're not far from a railroad track with fields on both sides of it. Our direction is parallel to the track, we must cross two fields to reach the woods ahead. On the other side of the track some horses are grazing but there's no farmhouse in sight. We are wading through the tall grass when there's a shout from Moses and white dandelion fuzz flies like dust as we dive headlong. I take a peek from the ground and see an orange trolley car chugging along the track spitting smoke. A man wearing suspenders and an old felt hat is riding it, I see him clearly through the waving stems of grass. The trolley slows and then stops. The driver appears to be looking at the horses, he is down the track from us and his back is turned. Then the trolley starts moving towards us, its motor put-put-putting, and halts again and it's directly opposite us and the man aboard is staring our way. I bury my face in the grass. After a minute he moves forward again, sliding down the track and around a bend.

"He couldn't see nothing. This grass is too deep," says Moses.

We are on our feet and further along wade through a sluggish brook and climb a creaking rusty wire fence, There are white blueberry blossoms by the fence and ferns and shrubs grow up the side of the railway embankment.

§

Perhaps the trolley didn't see us; but shortly after midday a helicopter does, and in this case there's no question about it. Because of the farms in the area we aren't always able to keep in the woods. It happens as we cross a hayfield, making for a rock fence that's thickly hedged by birch trees. A strong wind is in our faces (the sky now is black with thunder clouds) and we're slow to hear the helicopter approaching from behind. When its muffled staccato sound reaches our ears we make a run for it, in a sort of way. Always rough and impatient Moses hauls too hard on Brother Bell's leash, the preacher lurches forward on his face, and sprinting past them with my pack jolting up and down I hear Moses cursing. He gives a jerk on the rope that just about decapitates the preacher. "Get up, you—" Cavanaugh meanwhile is well back, stepping like a ballerina with no idea what's in front of him, more tip-toeing quickly than running. The helicopter is stuttering louder and louder but it's not yet in sight as I plunge into the cover of the birches. Liz comes in beside me but Cavanaugh and Brother Bell and Moses are still out in the open when the helicopter appears low and large over the trees drifting rapidly towards us. It's above the hayfield when Moses throws Brother Bell to the ground beside me, then reaches out for Cavanaugh and throws him on top of the preacher. The helicopter is so close I can feel the wind from its blades. It shoots on overhead and banks to the right and makes a narrow arc and passes over our heads again and flies off the way it came.

"You lousy bastard, Bell—" Brother Bell is coughing and choking—"I got a good mind to shoot you now instead of later. By Christ you fall down again like that and I'll rip your head clean off, so help me Jesus."

"My neck, brother... (cough, cough, choke)... "

"Now they know where we are! Now they know!"

"Did... did they see us?"

"Well, they saw *you*. That's for sure. Why didn't you run faster? Idiot!"

"I ran as fast as I could, Liz darling—"

"So *now* what?"

"Don't bother your heads about it. Fuck them. They can't do a damn thing while we got Bell."

We climb the stone fence and leave the birches and head off across another field.

"We'll stay in the woods after *this*," says Liz.

"We can't, goddammit, so shutup about it. We'd never get there in time. I'm using all the cover there is. We're about past this part of 'er anyways."

Cavanaugh's Beard

Sometime after three, when the open farm country is behind us and we are a couple of hours into the bush, we come to a rest by a small lake and have a quick meal of herring, beans and biscuits—we may not get another chance to eat until tomorrow, says Moses. But I find I'm not all that hungry, we're getting close to the mill, my stomach is anxious. I swallow what I can and then sit aside from the others. There's a forceful wind gusting off the lake, I turn my back to it and cup a match in my hands and light my pipe. I'm sitting smoking when Cavanaugh gropes his way to my side. He leans close and whispers, "Be on your guard... Moses is up to something. Did you hear him talk?... Pocket money and a new car... and what he implied, he'll try to get rid of me, he sees me as a threat... All of us going to Saint John, that's not right, we have to hold the countryside... And in Saint John—by now they must have our photographs, we're all on file, they'd have published them in the papers, we'll be recognized, they'll know because of the Chief and that LeBlanc fellow, they'll know it's us... I must make it to Montreal, go underground... from there I'll go into exile... he won't like that, he'll resist, he plans to spend the money himself, all will be lost..."

"What're you muttering about, you skinny prick?" Moses is standing over him. "Get on your feet and get marching."

"Our pictures... I was saying they'll recognize us in Saint John—as political prisoners you know they have our pictures ...."

"What do you think I been growing this beard for? I ain't growing it for nothing. I ain't shaved in four days." He rubs his hand over the dense black stubble; he's one of those types, like a hairy ape he can grow a beard in a week.

"That's what you ought to do, weak-eyes, grow a beard."

"But I already have a beard. I've always worn a beard."

"You call that a beard? That ain't no beard. I got more hair than that on the end of my cock." With a snort of laughter he walks away and grips his pack and throws it on his back. "Alright, enough arsing around, let's get on the road. We're not too damn far from that mill now, maybe a couple of miles, so watch yourselves. Keep your eyes open and your traps shut. It's mostly woods from here judging by the map.

§

What will they do?

They know where we made the phone call from, the woman at the farm would have told them that by now.

The helicopter saw us, and probably the man on the trolley.

They know where we're going: to the old mill to pick up the money.

Therefore they know the course we're following.

If they choose they can easily lie in ambush for us.

What's to stop them? The fate of our prisoner? Hah! Do they care about the life of one miserable preacher, or a hundred or a thousand Brother Bells? When their hold on power is at stake? When they have the chance to wipe out the very heart of our movement?

But they must think of the public's repugnance. If they sacrifice callously an innocent man's life the rising may spread yet more broadly and rapidly.

But... how much do the people know? Aside from the underground network who knows of us? Are the people even aware that we have a prisoner?

Could it be that the media is "cooperating" with them? It's happened before. Is it possible they've reported nothing and nobody but a handful of individuals is aware we exist? Or if our existence is known, are our motives? Our raison d'etre? And what have the police been told, who do they think they're to shoot at?

How much is known of us by anyone, for that matter, even the government? That ludicrous phone call of Moses could have conveyed little of our power, of our potential, of the magnitude of our threat.

No, in the end it comes down to the Chief... What, if anything, has he told them?

It must come down to that.

CHAPTER ELEVEN

Betrayal

I should have listened to my own logic.

But then I trusted the Chief.

We come to one enormous gouge in the woods after another, broad meadows of stumps and cut and tangled branches, the remains of a massive pulp cutting operation, and none of them are on Moses' map. The first few we skirt, a laborious and time-consuming process, certain to put us behind schedule, until Moses decrees that we're to proceed straight across them.

We reach the verge of yet another clearing.

"C'mon, pentecoster, get up here in front of me. Move." The storm clouds are rolling low and dark and the wind beats at the trees; it comes face onto us and leaning into it we start across.

Suddenly I'm being pushed back, Cavanaugh is

knocked against me by Moses. Liz snaps, "Watch where you're going!"

> *"Stop where you are!"*

"Who said that?" says Cavanaugh. "Who—"

> *"We have you covered! Drop your weapons!"*

The voice is high-pitched and screams nervously down the wind. We stand frozen still as statues. Where are they? I scan the far side of the clearing but can see nothing. "See what you did, Moses! Now what do we do?" says Liz accusingly. "Aaarrgh ..." The sound from Moses' throat is savage, barbarous. "I saw those bastards over there...Get ready." "What—what will we do?" Cavanaugh's voice trembles. "Do we put our hands up?" With a sudden movement Moses yanks viciously on the leash in his hand and hurls the preacher to the ground. Firing off a quick shot from the rifle he roars, "Start shooting!" and dives for cover behind a stump. He lands beside me for I'm already lying behind a stump and there's Cavanaugh in front of me on hands and knees quivering violently.

"Oh dear me! Oh my!"

For two seconds there's no reply and I hear our .303 clacking another round into the breach—and suddenly the air explodes with a colossal and deafening barrage of rifle fire—there must be a dozen automatic rifles blasting in rapid fire, and like a sudden hailstorm the shells come ripping through the leaves and slamming into the stumps. I lie paralyzed, glued to the earth and for a moment unable to think. Out of the corner of my eye I see Liz lying on her stomach; she's shucking her pack off her shoulders; she begins slithering the few yards back to the trees. Several shells smack the side of my stump—they are off to our left too. I realize I have to get moving. Like Liz I shrug out of my pack and squirm around on my stomach and scramble on elbows and knees for the trees. Because of the underbrush, the discarded branches, the columns of stumps, they are firing blind, trying to pulverize the area where they saw us take cover. In a reckless instant I reach a thick spruce tree across from Liz who is behind another one. Moses appears wriggling on his stomach out of the clearing, rifle in one hand and dragging his pack with the other. Once behind a tree he whirls and immediately starts returning fire. As fast as he can work the bolt he lets off round after round until the magazine is empty. He is fumbling for another one when the shooting from the other side subsides. There are a couple of isolated shots before it ceases altogether.

The voice that screamed before screams again:

"We have you surrounded You can't escape! Come forward with your hands up!"

"Go to hell!" Moses is craning his neck. He hollers, "Bell! Get the Jesus back here! Get back here or I'll blow your head off! Move you sonuvawhore!" I peer around the tree but I can't see the preacher, the underbrush is too thick. That means Moses can't see him either.

"I see you, Bell! Get back here! I'm gonna count to three—and if you don't get moving—"

"Give yourselves up! This is your last chance!"

"Go fuck yourself! One ..." At the roar of "two" Brother Bell is bluffed out, he springs up from among the stumps and starts running—only he's running away from us across the clearing, waving his arms and bellowing: "Praise Jesus, hold your fire! Don't shoot, it's me, it's me—he's going to kill me!"

"You goddamn—" Moses inserts a fresh magazine, looks quickly at me and reaches over and snatches the shotgun from out of my hands—without realizing it I've hung onto the thing—"This'll do better," he says.

Brother Bell is busily shouting and scrambling his way across the clearing when Moses, on one knee, takes aim and Whump! the preacher leaps into the air with a great howl and disappears down among the underbrush.

"Right in the arse," says Moses, passing back the shotgun.

A pained, outraged hoarse voice carries back to us: "You dirty Jew! Ohhhh... You bastard... Ohh—"

All at once a second barrage opens up at us. I keep pressed to the ground, but Moses pokes his head around the tree and fires off a shot from the .303. He jumps back, hit in the face by a chunk of flying bark. "We better shove off out of here."

It's hard to hear what he says. Through the uproar of gunfire I holler at him, "What about Cavanaugh?"

"The hell with him. We'll never get away with

that blind bastard. He's probably dead anyway."

There's a lull in the firing.

"Cavanaugh!" I shout.

"Here! Here! Wait for me! Where are you?"

I peek around the tree but can't see him.

"...this way!"

"I said fuck him," says Moses. "He'll slow us down."

"What are they doing?" Liz rises to her knees. She's holding the revolver which she hasn't used. "They aren't shooting so much now. They must be up to something."

"You're damn right they're up to something." I look in time to catch a glimpse of a uniformed figure dart behind a tree to the left of the clearing. "They're moving up. So let's—jumping Jesus ..."

Cavanaugh has suddenly popped up out of the underbrush and is standing there. He looks around blindly for an instant, then bent at the waist in a pathetic effort to hide himself he begins running—

"Not that way! Get down!"

"Wait for me! Where are you? Wait—"

He is running towards the side of the clearing, completely confused, running parallel to our position and towards the men moving up on our left. He hits a stump, reels, there's a sudden hard burst of firing and he goes down.

Moses is already moving on hands and knees back through the trees. "C'mon! This is our chance!" Crouched low we follow him and then we're on our feet and running. We run softly at first, trotting furtively, but the impulse for flight is too overpowering and in a minute we are racing through the bush with all restraints gone; we are routed, in headlong retreat, hurtling through branches and over fallen trees, clawing our way forward with the sound of gunfire in our ears. There's no telling how close behind us they are—or if they think we're still pinned down—and there may be more of them waiting up ahead; but in our disorderly flight we don't consider anything, we run until we can endure it no longer and panting and struggling for breath come to a staggering halt. The three of us stand with heads hanging down, not able to even speak for a moment. Then:

"D'you... hear anything?" Moses' massive chest heaves in and out, the pack on his back rising and falling with each breath. We listen but hear only the wind. Then there is the rumble of thunder.

They... they..." I have to fight back the urge to vomit... "mustn't have seen us go... Cavanaugh... they were busy shooting at him."

"That dummy ..." When he's recovered somewhat Moses says, "It'll soon be dark. If we keep clear of them till dark we'll be better off. Let's go. And don't talk or nothing, they'll be beating the bush looking for us."

The first drops of rain begin to fall. "Maybe Cavanaugh only tripped," I think. "He was bound to fall down by himself anyway."

We are not long on our way, taking our time

and walking carefully and stopping to listen every so often, before the rain comes down in earnest. Lightning splits the sky and there's a hard clap of thunder and we're soon drenched by a lashing rain; and long after the thunder has rumbled out of hearing the rain pours down and it continues throughout the night, almost to dawn, and we march the entire night splashing through it.

CHAPTER TWELVE

The End Of The Evaluation

Liz is looking at me sternly, she has a strange expression on her face, I noticed it in the last light of yesterday, she stared at me then with her lips tight together as though bitterly accusing me of something.

We have only the one sleeping bag, the one Moses held onto attached to his pack. He disappears into the trees and in a minute comes back, looks at Liz for a while and says, "You can use this," tossing the sleeping bag down beside her. But she shakes her head.

"You want to sleep on the wet ground?"

Again she shakes her head.

"I'm not going to sleep," she says. She's sitting cross-legged a few yards from me and she continues to stare at me fixedly.

"Suit yourself. I'll use it meself then."

He strips off his wet clothes until he's

completely naked. As I suspected he's covered all over with black hair, like a bear. From inside the sleeping bag he says, "At least we got rid of that creeping Jesus... Can't understand why we had him in the first place. He shoulda been on the street corner selling pencils." In a few seconds he's snoring loudly.

I don't feel sleepy right now. Soaked to the skin and exhausted I sit passively—like a sodden plant waiting for the sun to shine. I have a few simple thoughts in my head. Monotonously I go over them, as though they needed memorizing. I think that I will retain Moses... he knows his way through the woods... even if it means going as far as Saint John... Saint John... Yes, I'll go to Saint John... there I'll dismiss the two of them... there I must begin the job of rebuilding... Moses Saint John... rebuilding... I have the underground to draw upon... no shortage of fighting men... I must mould a new command unit... I'll dismiss the two of them... rebuild... and it's time now for me to shed my mask... my men... they must see and know their leader... for the decisive confrontation ahead... remove the mask... I can... accomplish nothing further... this way... tired of it... worn it too long... retain... Moses until Saint John... give them their discharge... new command unit... rally our forces... these are the crucial... days, the blackest days... I must have the strength... regroup our forces... turn the tide, I will do this... the fight... carry the fight to the enemy... don't say a word to them... reach Saint John... dismiss... them... the underground...

rendezvous... new... command... great offensive...

These thoughts go on and on, over and over in my fatigued mind....

§

It is burning hot and there's a brilliant red before my eyes and I wake beneath a scorching sun. For a moment I'm confused. I'm lying on the ground in the midst of a stand of poplar trees. I'm lying on wet grass and the sun is streaming through the leaves. It comes to me now... the ambush, the precipitous retreat, the rain, the incessant sodden marching, the dismal aspect of things in the cold morning twilight.

Liz is still sitting where she was before, still awake, blackened eyes still looking sternly at me. She's holding the revolver in her hand.

My eyes fall on Moses. He's stretched out on the sleeping bag with his pack beneath his head, he's awake and stark naked and his eyes are shining. One big hand is wrapped around a bottle.

"You're awake, are you?" he says. "You want a drink of rum? Well you can't have one, there's just enough for me and Liz... only she don't want her share so I guess I have to drink it." With a hoarse croak of laughter he raises the bottle to his mouth and gurgles down a drink. He exhales loudly.

"That's the stuff. I figure I earned a drink after all that tramping through the woods. Helps me to think. I been thinking... I been thinking we went at this whole business the wrong way... You can't make big money fucking around with some go-preacher from the sticks, nobody'd pay for the likes of him. You seen what they done shooting at us like that? They coulda hit him as easy as us but they didn't give a damn, they let go all the same... Makes you wonder... I'11 tell yez what we're gonna do, you listening? I been thinking it over... Next time we're gonna get one of them millionaires, some sonuvawhore who won't miss a hundred thousand bucks or so... there's a bunch of them in Saint John, all kinds of millionaires down there, thieves and crooks every one of them... You won't see no shooting when we get our hands on one of them bastards, nossir, you watch how fast they pay... they know who they're dealing with..."

He slugs back another drink and wipes his mouth with the back of his hand and says, "Wonder how that pentecoster is feeling now, I bet he ain't doing too much sitting around on his arse today." He lets out another guffaw. "Going on about that Bible stuff all the time, the jeezly fraud... that's right, eh Liz?... All them preachers are fucking frauds... Liz won't take a drink, don't know what's wrong with her... eh, what's—"

"SPY!"

Her piercing shriek makes my hair stand on end. Pale as a ghost she raises her arm and points the revolver at me. She shrieks again:

"SPY!"

Moses' voice is slurred: "What's that, Liz? Who's a spy?"

"Him! *He's* the spy! I've been watching him!"

So that's why she's been sitting there like that... Feeling my skin start to crawl I sit up, trying to think of something to say to her, to confront this hysteria—

"Don't move!"

"This is absurd—you don't—"

"Quiet! You thought you had me fooled, didn't you?

"I saw you smirking up your sleeve. You fooled the others—they were stupid—but you didn't fool me!"

"What're you talking about?" says Moses.

"Why do you think everything has gone wrong?" Her unblinking eyes are fastened on me. "Everything! First the Chief, then our political prisoner, then LeBlanc, now that ambush! How did they know where to wait for us? It wasn't that fool Cavanaugh. They shot *him*. And it's not Moses, no Moses wanted the fifty thousand too badly—no, it leaves only this traitor! He's been working for them from the start, he's a spy, a plant, an agent for our enemies!" The pistol is shaking in her hand.

"This is all in your imagination—Moses, tell—"

"It is not! Traitor!"

"How could I, I've been with the rest of you all the time—they shot at me too—I'm no spy, I'm—"

"You are so! You are so a spy! And you probably had a radio set in your pack and that's why you left it back there, you were afraid I was on to you!

And they didn't shoot at you, they just pretended to!"

"You left your pack, too."

"That's different! I'm not a spy and you are! Moses!"

"Yes, Liz me dear!"

"We must eliminate this traitor. He must be destroyed. You'll shoot him. The revolution goes on and traitors will not stand in the way. We are going to the capital to capture the Premier—"

"Hold on there, we're going to Saint John first, I told you that, we have to make some money... Tell you what, maybe we'll hold up a bank to start off, that's faster, and then we get ourselves a millionaire and after that we'll see what else we can do."

"Kill him! We have to kill him!"

I look out of the corner of my eye for the shotgun; it's leaning against a tree several feet away. Her eyes are fixed on me like a snake's. My mouth has gone dry as ashes. "Moses, tell her—"

"Silence! Traitor! I'll shoot you myself!" Her hand is trembling—perhaps she would miss if—

Moses stirs. "Liz me dear, take it easy, we can't go round firing guns or they'll hear us... can't go making noise..."

"Then strangle him!"

Moses gets unsteadily to his feet and comes towards us, rolling like a bear, a man twice my size. Between the two of them—I look quickly around—they have me cornered.

"Moses, for Godsake—" I say.

"Shutup."

In desperation I search for a way out. My shotgun—she would shoot before I reached it—get up and run she'll shoot—struggle with Moses—lunge at her now and hope she'll miss—I have to—

Moses suddenly snatches the pistol from her hand and laughs.

"Easy, Liz dear... never know who's around to hear a shot... Ha ha!"

"Kill him! Hit him over the head with it!"

"Why would I do that?"

"He's a spy!"

He sits clumsily down beside her and puts his gross hand on her leg. He hasn't a stitch of clothes on.

"He ain't no spy, that useless arsehole don't have the brains to be a spy." Ignoring me he lifts his hand off her leg and wraps a hairy arm around her shoulder. His hand drops down and envelopes one of her breasts. She doesn't move, she's still glaring at me.

"He is a spy! You'll be sorry if you let him get away!"

"Naw, he ain't no spy, don't be bothering your head about it. We got better things to do." He pulls her closer, changes hands with the pistol and with his free hand starts fumbling at the buttons of her shirt.

"I'll kill him myself! I'll kill him myself!"

He snorts with half-drunken laughter. "Whyn't you have a drink of rum... We're gonna have a good time when we get to Saint John, me and you, Liz... a real good time... get lotsa money... nice place to stay..." Now he is tugging at the belt on her bush pants. She continues to stare at me, not moving. Then—as though something just occurred to him—Moses turns his head my way and growls: "Okay, numb-nuts, get going, you ain't wanted around here. You heard what she said, she wants to kill you. We don't need you no more so fuck off. Get going and don't come back."

I am not slow getting to my feet. It would be folly to try and tell them anything. This is not the situation for Moses to suspect my real identity. For now let them enjoy their ignorance. They will know in time. How could she think—how could they fail to realize it was the Chief who turned against us? The Chief with his bitter hatred of the white race, all the time clandestinely plotting to pit both forces against each other, to weaken us both, to pave the way for the rising of the red man... I could have told her, if I'd been able to get a word in, but it would have done no good. In her frame of mind she'd never have accepted the truth, she couldn't believe the Chief would betray us. With her shaking finger on the trigger the wrong word would have been fatal, anything that might enrage her more... I had to be very careful.

Without another word I set off through the woods, for it's just as well I leave them now, I have no further use for them. A little way on I pause a moment and look back. Through the trees I see Moses climbing all over Liz, roughly pulling at her bush pants and growling like a wild animal. In a quiet voice I say:

"One day you'll know, one day you'll realize who was in your midst. Yes, one day you'll know what fools you've been." The next time I glance back they are hidden from sight and I put them out of my mind. On the landscape of history what are they? Mere specks of dust, insignificant, transitory, of no importance whatever.

EPILOGUE

For the next two days and nights I wandered through the wilderness completely lost, with no idea where I was or in which direction to point myself, possibly walking around in circles much of the time, as I understand happens in these circumstances. The hardships I endured can be imagined, I needn't describe them. Then, finally, on the afternoon of the third day, when I thought I'd never find my way out, I stumbled onto a secondary road. Making my way along this I reached a service station where I virtually collapsed from hunger and fatigue and thirst. My position was desperate. Indeed it was such that I was forced to take a gamble, and so I rashly told the service station attendant who I was, and requested his assistance.

In a tremorous, weakened voice I blurted out: "You see before you the leader... of the rebel forces... I am the Commander-in-Chief of the Popular Liberation Party... My friend, how goes the war? Are you one of us... Will you help me?... Central Command was ambushed, some of us were wiped out, a few panicked, turned against their leader... against everything the cause stands for... I must reach the underground... are you with me?"

He looked at me in a puzzled way, as though I was delirious. And perhaps to some extent I was, after the exertions and deprivations of the past few days. Had I been stronger I would not of course have taken such a risk. If only... If he had been one of us, a member of the underground, or even a sympathizer! But it was too much to hope for. He merely acted bewildered, even a little frightened. Admittedly I was a strange sight to look upon, ragged and unshaven and filthy. When I saw his unpromising reaction I tried to laugh as though I'd been joking.

He gave me some water, and when I drank it I tried to continue on but was physically unable. I recollect an ambulance coming, I drifted into a deep sleep, and when I awoke they were there. The garage attendant, either through ignorance or malice to our cause, had given me away. Despite my feeble condition I fought to the end, I strove to escape from them but I was outnumbered and soon overpowered.

Thus it is today that I find myself in captivity. From here I am forced to conduct as best I can the struggle outside. But I have not lost hope, not by any means. I know that one day soon I shall be freed, that the hour is fast approaching when the doors will be flung open and I will step forward to march with my fellow soldiers to victory. That, I know, is inevitable.

AFTERWORD

*Excerpt from an interview at the
online book site Salty Ink*

A Quick Chat with Prolific New Brunswick author Raymond Fraser, the man with five books in Clare & Adams' *Atlantic Canada's 100 Greatest Books.*

In 2009 Fraser won the the inaugural Lieutenant-Governor's Award for High Achievement in English Literary Arts, a $20,000 award designed to "recognize the outstanding contribution of individuals to the arts." He also released his eighth novel in 2009, *In Another Life*, of which Leap Magazine said "think *Catcher in the Rye* meets Hemingway and Bukowski."

SALTY INK: Tell us about *The Struggle Outside*

RAYMOND FRASER: There's quite a long story behind it which I'll just touch on. I started it in

1969 at the time the Tupamaros guerillas were kidnapping politicians in Uruguay as one of their revolutionary tactics. I'm not sure why, perhaps because of the anomaly of it, but I thought it would be interesting to introduce a fictional movement of a similar kind to my home province of New Brunswick—start writing it and see where it led. I finished a version in Montreal in 1970, and while it was probably good enough by Governor General's Award or Nobel Prize standards it wasn't up to my own standards, so I put it aside and went back to it in 1972. I worked on it in the summer of '72 in a tent in Bay du Vin, New Brunswick, and continued it during the winter of 1972-73 in Spain and finished it over the summer of 1973 on an old boat I owned on the Miramichi River. I completely dismantled the first version and re-did it sentence by sentence, slowly and carefully, making the characters and scenes as vivid as possible in a somewhat surrealistic atmosphere—what you might call surrealistic realism (as life often is). While I was working on this second version, the well-known Canadian author Hugh Garner, who had read my first fiction book, *The Black Horse Tavern,* wrote me via my publisher Ingluvin Publications to say he considered me one the best young writers of my generation and offered to recommend my next book to his publisher, McGraw-Hill Ryerson. I thought that was extremely kind of him, and thanked him, and when *The*

Struggle Outside was ready sent it to his publisher and the editor there said he loved it and they would publish it and he kept telling me this and then one day a year later the manuscript came back in the mail with a note saying he was sorry but they weren't going to so it after all. I was naturally none too happy about that and wrote a detailed account of what I considered an outrage and sent it around the country including to the president of McGraw-Hill Ryerson who wrote back apologizing for how I'd been treated and asked to have another look at the novel. So I sent it a second time, and the upshot was they gave me a thousand dollar advance and published it in hardcover the next year, 1975. When it came out they had me up to Toronto where I did a number of TV and print interviews and I think the book sold about 1,200 copies and then disappeared.

As to how I came to revise *that* version... In 1975 there were no home computers that I was aware of, just typewriters, and I knew if I ever wanted to get *The Struggle Outside* reissued one day I'd need an electronic copy. To do that I had to scan it, and when I was correcting the scanned pages I made a number of changes I'd long felt were needed as well as some others that came to me as I went along. They weren't major alterations – mostly polishing up the writing and correcting topographical flaws; but they were enough that I'm glad I made them. This edition (which is also the one that appeared in my book *The Trials Of Brother Bell*) is now the official definitive edition.

A Note On The 3rd Edition

Among other changes this edition has dropped the first edition's awkward subtitle of "A funny serious novel". Having a subtitle on the book was never my idea. The publisher called me as the book was getting ready to go to the printer and said they needed a subtitle immediately and could I give them one. On such short notice I couldn't think of anything, so they went ahead and put one on themselves. It's been an aggravation over the years and I'm glad to be finally rid of it.

Raymond Fraser is the author of
eleven books of fiction, three of non-
fiction, and six collections of poetry.
His novel *The Bannonbridge Musicians*
was runner-up for the Governor
General's Award. In 2009 following
publication of his novel *In Another Life*
he received the Lieutenant-Governor's
Award for High Achievement in the
Literary Arts. He was appointed to the
Order of New Brunswick in 2012 for
his contributions to literature and
culture in the province.
http://raymondfraser.blogspot.com